SEE NO EVIL

JAMILA GAVIN

SEE NO EVIL

FARRAR, STRAUS AND GIROUX
NEW YORK

To Niema, with love

Copyright © 2008 by Jamila Gavin
All rights reserved
First published in Great Britain,
under the title *The Robber Baron's Daughter*, by Egmont UK Limited, 2008
Printed in the United States of America
Designed by Jay Colvin
First American edition, 2009

1 3 5 7 9 10 8 6 4 2

www.fsgteen.com

Library of Congress Cataloging-in-Publication Data
Gavin, Jamila.
   [Robber baron's daughter]
   See no evil / Jamila Gavin.— 1st American ed.
       p.   cm.
   Originally published: Robber baron's daughter. United Kingdom : Egmont, 2008.
   Summary: Twelve-year-old Nettie's sheltered and privileged life changes after her beloved tutor mysteriously disappears and Nettie, aided by the son of a household employee, begins to learn the truth about her father, whose wealth began with trafficking in illegal aliens.
   ISBN-13: 978-0-374-36333-8
   [1. Wealth—Fiction.   2. Family life—England—Fiction.   3. Household employees—Fiction.   4. Bulgarians—England—Fiction.   5. Illegal aliens—Fiction. 6. Espionage—Fiction.   7. Organized crime—Fiction.   8. London (England)— Fiction.   9. England—Fiction.]   I. Title.

PZ7.G2355See 2009
[Fic]—dc22

2008005123

Contents

SEE NO EVIL

1

Memories and Secrets

A figure came out of the darkness. He stood in the hall; motionless; breathless still; silent as space. A dim light caught his shadow and it began to expand and grow, blotting out the light, as if Satan himself had spread his wings, creating a black hole which was devouring the whole house.

"I want to know more about you. As far back as you can go," said Nettie's new tutor.

Far back . . . earliest memories . . . back and back. Sounds and images swirled in her head as she put pencil to paper, and she seemed to disintegrate. She was stardust again—that's how Miss Kovachev, her previous tutor, had described her. "Antonietta Roberts, you are nothing but *stardust*." Nettie could hear her voice now—high, sometimes edgy, as if she might burst into tears any minute, other times tinkling with laughter and excitement. "Out there in the universe, stars have been exploding forever," Miss Kovachev had whispered with awe. They often stood on the balcony of Nettie's bedroom, which looked out across the park, gazing up at the night sky, sometimes gasping at the sight of a shooting star.

"Who knows what they've seen, these stars: fire flaring for thousands of miles, a maelstrom of meteors hurtling past, huge torrents of rocks and boulders tumbling through space in an eternal flood. Throughout aeons of time, stardust has been sprinkling through the cosmos, landing on other planets, mixing with all sorts of minerals, and gases, creating life; dinosaurs, pterodactyls, lungfish; creating you. You are made up of all the elements in stars: hydrogen, calcium, iron, magnesium, salt; 0.005 of you is seawater. It's all carbon: all living things are made of carbon, and carbon comes from stars. Antonietta, you are made of stardust."

"I hope I won't be dusted up by the old woman who swept the cobwebs from the sky." Nettie had giggled, humming the nursery rhyme as she bent over her exercise book. She had tried to think how it would feel to be stardust; whether she could remember whirling through the universe until, caught in the gravitational pull of the earth, she had descended like fine rain, gleaming silver and gold in the dawn light, some of her particles falling on land, still steaming with heat from exploded volcanoes; some of her falling into water: deep, dark, unfathomable water. "Was I alive?" she had asked Miss Kovachev.

"You were neither alive nor dead. You were life."

Life—even the solid things of the house seemed alive: the walls, the water pipes, the hollow spaces behind the wooden panels, and the staircase winding around the hollow heart of the house, all seemed to breathe, observe, listen; all seemed to mutter and gossip among themselves with creaks and groans, gurgles and knocks, as if conferring with each other.

And the Boy understood.

————

"You won't get anything written with your pencil hanging in the air," her new tutor chided as she stared into space. "Come on, there must be something you remember."

His name was Don. Funny that she had always called Miss Kovachev "Miss Kovachev." She had never known what her first name was—and then she was gone. Nettie hadn't seen her go; saw no suitcase ready to be packed—and no one told her why, or where, and she still didn't know what her first name had been. But she was to call this one "Don," and was never to know his last name.

Somehow, she didn't want to tell Don about her memories, or her secrets. *She certainly wouldn't tell him about the Boy.*

"Can you remember being in your pram?" asked Don, trying to sound encouraging, but Nettie saw him glance at his watch as he asked her.

Miss Kovachev's voice would have been probing, inviting her to explore her memories, with all the excitement of travelers discovering new countries, rivers, jungles, or outer space. But Don's voice was dispassionate. It was a task for him that needed to be done, and she found his lack of enthusiasm left her blank, and her memories stifled.

Yet she knew that in the chambers of her brain, there were thousands of memories. She could go back to when everything was above her head: sounds of voices, laughter, discussions, arguments, anger, tears, and, sometimes, the soft words of making up. She seemed always to be looking upwards. Looking up at the grownups was like looking up at the sky, making out shapes and faces in the clouds. And when she was lying in bed, faces swam into her sight. Her mother in shining silks, her pretty face smooth as alabaster; somehow always backlit, the edges of her dark red hair dancing with lights as she bent to smother her with perfumed kisses in a good-night embrace. Sometimes her father came in too, and she would giggle and wriggle, trying to escape his tickling hands. Darling Daddy; he was so handsome and kind—everyone said so, and Mother grumbled and pouted because so many women liked him for his strong athletic figure, his long swept-back light brown hair, his smoky blue eyes, his elegant courtesy, and the way he made you feel the center of the universe when he talked to you. But everyone agreed he was such a good father.

As long as she could remember, there had been those grownup parties her parents were always throwing, wherever they were in the world. Ever since she was a young child, Nettie had been sneaking out of bed to spy on everyone, peering through banisters, edging her way step by step down staircases, and hiding behind pillars or potted plants.

Sometimes they spotted her, and laughed. "What are you up to, little Nettie?" they exclaimed. And if they came upon her eavesdropping on a conversation, they would hold up a warning finger and say, "Hush! Little pitchers have big ears." She knew that meant her—and the more she felt adults had secrets, the more she wanted to know.

As she grew older, she got to know that Olga, the cook, secretly liked her vodka, and often drank it straight from the bottle; that Gimley, the butler, had a girlfriend, who waited for him on his days off; that Ella, her own personal maid, sometimes cried when no one was looking, because she loved Tamas but he didn't love her; and Mrs. Bainbridge, the housekeeper, waged war on everyone.

Tamas was her mother's bodyguard. Nettie called him "Swivel-Eyes," because whenever they went out Tamas came, too, always a little behind, looking as if he wasn't with them, his eyes constantly on the move, scanning faces, doorways, windows, and rooftops. He was like one of those cameras you find in banks, always watching, always panning smoothly and silently, all the way through ninety degrees then back again.

But sometimes, as Nettie wandered unnoticed, knee high, and later waist high, among her parents' friends, she picked up snatches of conversation which she didn't completely understand: that Tommy just went and blew fifty grand at the casino last night, or that Marky came through with another *consignment*—whatever that meant, or that the price of shares in commodities was dancing a bit, or that Lenny gave Marissa a hundred-thousand-pound diamond necklace for her birthday, and she was still discontented with her marriage!

Her father was called Vlad, short for Vladimir, and sometimes his name was mentioned in undertones, as if they didn't want to be heard. "Vlad impaled that soft-bellied idiot. He had it coming to him," Nettie once heard, but Nanny came and whisked her away to bed.

As she grew older, Nettie was allowed to appear before the guests, all dressed up like a princess, and everyone would come over to pat her head, stroke her cheeks, and give her hugs and kisses. And Daddy would say proudly, "This is my greatest asset—along with Peachy." He drew his wife and daughter into the curved clasp of each arm, while everyone sighed and smiled to see such family bliss.

But though she still listened, and asked questions, no one was able to tell her where Miss Kovachev had gone. Somehow, there would be a strain in the air if she spoke her name, which Nettie detected but couldn't understand. *Well if they wouldn't tell her where Miss Kovachev was, she wouldn't tell them about the boy she had seen sneaking and creeping around.*

"You must at least be able to remember moving into Regent Mansion," suggested Don, with exaggerated patience. "Write this down, and then carry on: 'I remember the first time I saw Regent Mansion, and I thought it was . . .' "

"Horrible," wrote Nettie. "That's what I thought it was going to be. It had no swimming pool, no tennis courts, no Jacuzzi in the bathroom, no hot tub in the garden . . ." She came to a stop again, and remembered her father's words. "This will be our pad in London," he had said when he had shown her the house.

More like a dark castle, Nettie thought at first. Yet, though she had lived in villas in Sicily, chalets in Switzerland, apartments in Paris, bungalows in Bermuda, and their high-as-the-stars skyscraper apartment in New York, she had never lived in a town house as darkly mysterious as this, with four main floors linked by a winding staircase and an elevator which ascended all the way up to a penthouse apartment. As she set out to explore, she felt a strange quiver of excitement, as though she was discovering a new land.

They had stood in the center of the checkered floor of the lobby; gloomy, empty, and echoing, their voices resonating. Nettie had looked up into the circular atrium, up and up, her eyes following the dusty, coiling oak banister spiraling and diminishing as it rose higher. The ceiling at the top was domed with grimy glass, and dust drifted slowly in the shadowy light. On that first day, she had leaped up the stairs, compelled to follow the banister, as if it had magical properties and was luring her to the top. She rushed in and out of empty rooms, opening paneled cupboards, discovering shutters, which swung aside like fans, and interconnecting doors which led into unexpected rooms.

She had reached the top and burst into the empty penthouse apartment, and frozen at the sight of a wall of windows, high as a bird, through which London spread before her. Beyond the wide sweeping greenery of the park, with its trees and flower beds and winding walks, she glimpsed the distant Post Office Tower pointing upwards in an eastern sky above spires and office blocks, hotels and residences, in a rising and falling skyline; and, though she couldn't see it, she knew that farther beyond, winding through the city like a gleaming serpent, was the river Thames. She had crept forward till she had stood with her hands pressed up against the glass, feeling she could burst through into space. After that she had flying dreams.

But the room she loved best, and wanted for herself, was the round room in the tower. She had found it by groping up some dark side steps between the third and fourth floors, which she almost missed in her exploration. There was a door at the top. She tried the handle. Her fingers hesitated for a split second before she turned it. What would she find: an old lady sitting at a spinning wheel? Or Rapunzel, imprisoned by a wicked witch? Or might there be something more terrible, like the murdered wives in the secret locked room in Bluebeard's castle?

She stepped inside with held breath. It was dark and gloomy, and yet full of a strange enchantment. Everything was round: the walls were round, the ceiling was round, and the floor was round. It was like standing in the very center of everything; like the pupil in the center of an eye, or a hub in the center of a wheel. She felt she was at the very heart of the whole world, and that she could feel it rotating in space.

Only the windows, instead of being round, were slits like the windows you find in castles. Perhaps archers had once guarded the house, peering out of the narrow openings with their bows fitted, and the arrows resting on the sill, ready to be fired. Daylight shone through the slits and threaded across the bare wooden floor.

When she peered through the slits, though they were narrow she found she could see the park in almost every direction, and the streets beyond, and the broad sky as wide as an ocean, in which silver airplanes circled like sharks before diminishing into the distance as they hunted for their airport runway.

The room made her quiver with strange excitement. *I wish this could be mine,* she thought, and ran back down to her parents to stake a claim.

"We'll see, darling," soothed Peachy. "Whatever room you have, it will be beautiful, I promise you."

"Only the best for my darling daughter," said Daddy, laughing.

The Boy resented them coming. This house was his territory. He didn't want to give it up. He knew every inch: its cellars and attics, its cupboards and pantries; he moved in and out of its rooms, up and down its stairways; he knew its secrets and understood its language. Creeping through dark passages, or passing through rooms dusty with sunbeams, he sensed the spirits of past owners. They were watching, too, just as he had watched the renovation begin—to make this old house new.

He tried sabotage. When teams of builders, electricians, plumbers, and carpenters took over he teased them, threw them into confusion, and laughed at them when they began to ask fearfully, "Is this a haunted house?" How could the tins of cream paint get moved to the room which was being painted green? Who messed up the paintbrushes? Who unrolled the wallpaper and left it spread across the floor? Who removed the hammer from the tool kit in the kitchen and put it in the bath? And who upset Bill, the electrician, who, when he found all his lightbulbs had been unscrewed and placed unbroken on the floor beneath the sockets, walked out. "Not staying here. It's spooked!"

———

But in the end, it all got done, and by the time Nettie moved in the house had finally been transformed. It was like a palace. The gloom had been banished. The dingy hall floors had been replaced by glistening white marble, flanked by Grecian-style columns, and the ceilings hung with dangling crystal chandeliers; light and color glowed throughout, reflecting in mirrors, dancing on Persian and Turkish carpets, and illuminating a rainbow of satin cushions scattered on sofas, armchairs, and beds. Walls and woodwork had been painted in light creams, sunshine yellows, and earthy browns; other walls were covered in wallpaper of coiling leaves and exotic birds, and a bold, red velvet carpet rippled up four flights of stairs, gleaming in between the polished oak banisters.

It was a game. The Boy crept out to inspect what had been done and spy on the new owners. He tested the chairs and sofas, lay on the beds, turned on the showers, and wallowed in the Jacuzzi. He went to every floor, examining how each room had been designed and fitted for its particular function.

Mrs. Bainbridge, the housekeeper, was beside herself. Someone had left all the lights on in the sleek new kitchen; someone had switched on the blender, which she found going around and around with nothing in it. In the dining room, someone had muddled up the silver cutlery, mixing the fish forks with the meat forks and the soupspoons with the teaspoons, which she had so carefully set for dinner on the vast walnut table, and someone had thought it very funny to turn upside down the traditional French gold-gilt armchairs in her lady's magnificent drawing room, and scatter the sofa cushions across the floor. She was sure it was Nettie, but Nettie, the adored one and only child, was one person she couldn't touch even though she thought she was a spoiled little thing.

Mrs. Bainbridge was exasperated and complained to Nanny George. "For goodness' sake, control that child."

Nanny wasn't at all convinced it was Nettie, and suggested it was probably one of the new young manservants, but she did question Nettie's personal maid, Ella, about it, who just shrugged with bewilderment. Nettie herself denied all knowledge.

"Nettie may be a little spoiled," Nanny reported back to Mrs. Bainbridge, "but she doesn't lie."

However, despite the unexplained mischief, no harm was ever done, and the house soon looked as distinguished as any in England with its spacious rooms, adorned with ornaments and paintings: here a Picasso, over there a David Hockney, in an alcove a Vermeer, and over the mantelpiece a Monet. Nettie's father loved to be thought a cultivated man, and often attended the art auctions in New York, Paris, or London.

On every landing, in every room, were vases festooned with flowers. Mother always said, "I must have flowers," and every day, the flower van arrived, and the maids brought in armfuls of English roses, lilies and gardenias from Kenya, or orchids freshly flown in from Thailand, their perfume invading the house. Luckily, it was Gimley who came across the newly delivered irises scattered across the marble floors of the hallway, otherwise someone's head would have rolled. He did wonder whether Cook was right about the house being haunted.

The old elevator had been ripped out, and a new glass lift rose like a bubble, up one side of the atrium, passing the largest chandelier of all—a vast, shimmering constellation of crystal droplets, which hung on a looped iron chain, as thick as a ship's anchor, lighting up all four floors. Once, before they had moved in, one of the night guards saw the elevator rising silently upwards, empty, as though someone had summoned it, only to descend, still empty.

The first thing Nettie had done, the day they moved in, was to get into the lift, counting the floors as it carried her up to the top. She inspected Vlad and Peachy's apartment: their own private suite of rooms with bedroom, living room, study, kitchen, and bathroom, now sumptuously furnished with soft white carpets, delicate embroidered curtains, and mirrors held by golden cherubs. She tried out their vast bed, lying spread-eagled, feeling as if she could just float out of the windows and sleep among the clouds.

But when she was told which was to be her own suite of rooms on the third floor, she couldn't help giving a groan of disappointment. Even though they were light and airy: her bedroom, her sitting room, bathroom, playroom, and study, all painted and decorated in white and her favorite rose pink; even though she had tall French windows, with soft billowing curtains of white and pink, which opened onto a wrought-iron balcony festooned with wisteria and climbing rose; and even though her rooms all overlooked the park, she couldn't help exclaiming with regret, "Oh! I did so want the Round Tower!"

"Darling, it's far too small for you, and cut off from the rest of the house," explained her mother. "We don't like you being out on a limb and so separate from all of us. Anyway, it's such a dark, gloomy room. I'm sure you'd have bad dreams. That's why we've given you this lovely, sunny suite, and you've got Nanny adjoining you so you won't be lonely."

"But who will have the Round Tower?" Nettie sighed.

"That will be for Miss Kovachev."

2

Miss Kovachev

Nettie would never forget the day Miss Kovachev came to be her tutor.

Although she was a young woman, she seemed strangely old-fashioned. The day she arrived, she wore a longish, dull maroon skirt with a high-necked blouse and plain sensible shoes. Her pale, angular face was solemn and shy, but not unpleasant. She wasn't wearing any jewelry or makeup, not like Nettie's mother, who, with her personal lifestyle guru, Chantal, always spent at least an hour each day choosing her clothes, "putting on her face," and selecting exactly the right jewelry. "I never go out without a necklace, bracelet, and earrings," Peachy would say, "otherwise I feel quite naked."

Nettie had insisted on being the one to show Miss Kovachev her room in the Round Tower. They went up in the lift to the third floor, and climbed the small flight of steps which led to the arched wooden door. As Miss Kovachev stepped inside, Nettie gazed into her face to see her reaction. Would it be the same as hers? Was that not a flicker of pleasure as she looked at the round room with its newly painted pale watery green plastered walls, offset with a white plastered ceiling, white painted baseboards, and tasteful fabrics

specially chosen by Peachy to blend in with her color scheme?
Everything in the room was rounded; the sofa, the dresser, the
bookshelves, the display cabinets, and even the bed fitted into the
rounded curves. Two of the slit windows had been widened to give
more light, and were hung with thin, white Swiss-embroidered curtains. Light rippled in as if entering a dappled, leafy woodland pool.

"Do you love it?" Nettie asked eagerly. "I do. I wanted it, but
wasn't allowed."

"Yes," replied the young woman quietly. "I love it." She spoke in a
soft voice, yet with a strangely sharp-edged accent which wasn't
British.

"Do you feel like Rapunzel?"

"A little bit." Miss Kovachev smiled. "Though I don't think my
hair is long enough to reach down to the ground if I lean out of the
window. Even when I was your age and it grew right down to my
bottom, it wouldn't have reached the ground!"

No, Miss Kovachev's hair was not long enough to reach the
ground, but it seemed to have a life of its own: full and lustrous
black, swinging with every move of her head, tossing on her shoulders like a shining wave. "Oh well!" she joked. "That means I won't
get any prince climbing up to visit me," and they both laughed.
From then on Nettie adored her, and knew they would be the best
of friends.

Come to think of it, thought Nettie, twiddling her pencil, it was
Miss Kovachev who was most like stardust, even though Peachy
had remarked that she was "a bit of a mouse" and wasn't much to
look at—her nose was too long, and her mouth rather unruly as if
from rolling too many words around her tongue. But Nettie thought
she was beautiful. She was slender, pale—phantasmal even; her face
was gentle and kind, as someone who is good is also kind, and when

her coal black eyes burned with intensity, or if she burst out laughing, everything lit up like fireworks.

Paul, one of their domestic staff, had brought up a single large shabby suitcase and plonked it down in the middle of the room. "There you are, miss," he said in a dutifully polite voice, and backed out shutting the door behind him.

"May I watch you unpack?" Nettie had asked her that day.

"I haven't much to show you." Miss Kovachev smiled.

Nettie watched her closely as she hung up two rather dull skirts and blouses, two plain dresses, one pair of gray slacks—all very unfashionable—and set her three pairs of shoes in a row. *Not like Mama,* she thought, who had a separate dressing room with a walk-in closet the length of one whole wall, filled with row upon row of dresses and skirts, blouses and slacks, and rack upon rack of shoes: high heels, sandals, espadrilles, in colors to go with any outfit she might choose that day.

And Miss Kovachev seemed to have nothing to put in her cabinets. The shelves and windowsills stayed curiously empty: no photographs, no ornaments, no knickknacks—as though no one had ever given her anything—unlike Nanny's room, in which every possible space was cluttered with family photographs, and with what Peachy called "junk." Miss Kovachev simply came with a handful of shabby books which stood on the bookshelves: well-thumbed dictionaries, poetry books—some written in a language Nettie couldn't understand—and an out-of-date laptop computer. When she had finished unpacking, Miss Kovachev went to the window and gazed out, looking suddenly as wistful as a bird in a cage. Nettie thought she saw tears glistening in her eyes. Nettie asked her why her shelves were so bare, and Miss Kovachev replied, in her odd, high foreign voice: "Possessions are a hindrance. The fewer you have the better. You come into this world with nothing, and you will leave with nothing—even if you are an Egyptian pharaoh. So why clutter up your life with things you don't need? I want to be like a bird: I'll make my nest, have food and shelter, but I can fly away whenever I want."

So, thought Nettie bitterly, twirling her pencil around her fingers. The Round Tower was no different from a bird's nest, and when Miss Kovachev had had enough, she just flew away. *She can't have loved me after all.*

"Well?" Don's voice broke into her thoughts. "You won't get anything done with your pen bobbing in the air like that. Look!" He stared at the open page. "You've only written one sentence—and not a very nice one at that, beginning with the word 'horrible.' What is horrible? Are you going to write about it, eh?" He almost smiled.

"I'm still thinking."

"Tch!" His almost smile contracted back into his tightened jaw. He clicked his tongue with frustration, as if teaching a young, rather dull child was not what he had been put on God's earth for.

"We've only a few more minutes, tell me about Miss Kovachev. Would you have described her, too, as *horrible?*"

"Oh no!" Nettie exclaimed. And then felt embarrassed as if she had implied that Don was horrible in comparison, though she did find him nondescript. Brown, she thought. His color is brown, what hair he has is brown, his eyes are brown, his specs are brown-rimmed, his jacket, trousers, and shoes are brown; dull as ditchwater, as Nanny would say.

But this house horrible? "I thought it was when I first saw it," she wrote, "but then . . ."

How could she write about how the house had become her playground? She felt she would never discover all of it, there were so many rooms. She loved prowling through them like a cat; silently crouching behind sofas, hiding in the folds of those heavy embroidered satin curtains, listening to conversations, playing games about being a secret agent who had to obtain urgent documents from a drawer, or a top secret message hidden in a vase. Sometimes she fancied she was a prisoner, being held by a wicked king like Bluebeard. Perhaps there were secret rooms.

And then there was the Boy. She had seen him from the day they moved in. At least, she thought there was a boy. She wasn't sure if he was real. He never stood long enough for her to see him properly. It didn't matter. She had often made up imaginary friends. When she played her spying games, she pretended he was there, her secret friend—or enemy? She hadn't decided, but a secret for sure. She hadn't told anyone—not even Miss Kovachev when she came. So she certainly wouldn't write about him, otherwise he wouldn't be a secret anymore. She stopped again.

"Nettie?" Don's voice was weary. "Why have you stopped this time?"

"Don't know. I think of something to write, but by the time I've put down one sentence, it's all vanished, and I don't know what to say."

He seemed disconcerted by her uncooperative pout, running his fingers compulsively through his thinning hair as if to check that he still had some. His hands swooped around his skull, then down his neck, like two birds in a mating dance. They entwined and crossed, and each hand began to massage his upper arms, and make their way down to his elbows and forearms to his wrists. His fingers fluttered, as if with a mind of their own, which guided them back to his skull, and the whole procedure started again.

Nettie thought he reminded her of someone or something, but she wasn't sure what. Her pen doodled in the margin, her thoughts racing ahead, faster than she could write ... and anyway, she didn't feel like telling Don how she remembered being puzzled as to why Miss Kovachev came with so little.

He looked disappointed. She knew he thought she was sulking. She lowered her gaze to the empty page. She refused to look him in the eye, smile, or try to please him. Inside, she was furious and grief-stricken all at the same time, because no one had told her that Miss Kovachev was leaving, and she hadn't even said goodbye. Why hadn't they told her? Who had decided it? Why hadn't she been consulted? She felt betrayed, not just by her mother and father, but by Miss Kovachev herself. Why hadn't she said anything? *Just because I'm a child, they think I don't count,* she raged to herself.

Miss Kovachev had never been like the other young women: those au pairs and maids who had come and gone as if on a conveyor belt. She had stayed; stayed with her for over a year—and Nettie had thought she would stay forever. The others hadn't mattered—not as she had mattered. The others hadn't been her friend, or cared about her like Miss Kovachev. She had made no concession to her being a child, but always addressed her as an equal.

Learning with Miss Kovachev had never been boring. They went on walks, naming trees and flowers, looking at clouds and learning how they were made and what they were called; they went to museums and exhibitions; they looked up words neither of them knew, and surfed the Internet to learn about places they had never been to. Even math was a game. Time meant nothing. Everything was as short or as long as it needed to be. Miss Kovachev sometimes got so excited—whether it was over a poem, a tree, a story, or a constellation in the night sky—that she would almost stand on tiptoe, look-

ing as if she would levitate; fly; and it was Nettie who would clasp
her hand in case she got left behind.

Was that what had happened? Had Miss Kovachev suddenly
found the skill to fly? Was she up there in the stars, gathering stardust?

After she left, Nettie had entered Miss Kovachev's room in the
Round Tower, hoping there might be something there to give her a
clue. Everything looked the same: the round furniture, the specially
made bed; and yet it wasn't the same. The room was not just bare—
it had always been bare; there was a sense of emptiness, like a shell
is empty, like Grandpa's body had been empty after death.
Although his body was there, he, the person she loved, had gone,
and Nettie had felt that plunging loneliness. Now Miss Kovachev
had gone, too. Her presence was no longer there: her faint waft of
scented soap no longer hung in the air, no book rested on the side
table opened at the point where she had stopped, and no computer
was open on the desk.

Nettie had rushed to Nanny's apartment. "Why, Nanny? Why has
she gone? Why did no one tell me?"

But Nanny was strangely reticent. She just shrugged. "Sorry,
child. I don't really know beyond hearing that she had to go and
deal with a family matter." And she had changed the subject.

Ah! thought Nettie, with sudden understanding. That's it. A family matter. Probably someone in Miss Kovachev's family was ill,
maybe even dying. Only something so serious would make her leave
without even saying goodbye. And yet . . . and yet . . . she couldn't
accept that Miss Kovachev hadn't even had the time to give her a
hurried kiss—just a whisper of goodbye, a rushed murmur of why,
where, and, most of all, if she would return. She waited for a letter
or just an e-mail, but nothing came.

At least Don wasn't given the Round Tower when he moved in to take Miss Kovachev's place as her tutor. He had expressed a desire for a more spacious apartment, and was given rooms on the other side of the atrium.

Don looked at his watch again. "We'll call it a day." He said it with a sigh. "But for your homework, I'd like you to write at least a page under the heading 'Memories.' Perhaps you'll remember more when you're on your own in your study. Memories are always good material for when you write stories or poems. All I'm trying to do is find out what you are capable of, don't you see?" Once again, his hands went to his head, massaging his bald patch, winding around his neck, reaching between his shoulder blades, and moving back down his arms and wrists.

Suddenly Nettie knew what he reminded her of—he was like a preening monkey. She convulsed with giggles. She would never be able to look at Don now without thinking of a monkey. She would call him Don the Chimp.

He frowned questioningly, wondering what she had suddenly found so funny, but not being let in on the joke, shoveled a sheaf of papers into his briefcase and made for the door, leaving Nettie still shaking with suppressed laughter. "See you tomorrow," he muttered.

"See you," echoed Nettie like a peewit. "See you!" Its call soared inside her head, and she remembered that Miss Kovachev had also told her that she was 0.005 seawater.

"I'm made out of stars and seawater, did you know that? You, too, Don the Chimp." She stopped laughing.

3

The Ghost

ecause Nettie's mother loved light, she loved mirrors. There were small mirrors and large mirrors, huge gilt mirrors, horizontal mirrors, and oval mirrors. They glimmered along gloomy corridors, and at the tops of stairways. There were mirrors in every room reflecting light and shadows.

It was in one of these mirrors that Nettie once again glimpsed a shape as she hung over the banisters, wondering how to pass the time. Down below on the second floor, it moved, and crept, and darted from a curtain to a pillar, then vanished. *It was a boy. Not a shadow or a trick of the light, this time she was certain, it was a boy—wasn't it? Her heart nearly jumped out of her body. But what was a boy doing in the house? Who was he? Where had he gone? Quick—catch up with him. She scuttled down the stairs as fast as she could. The corridor was empty. Where could he be? In Great-aunt's apartment?*

Great-aunt Laetitia had arrived soon after Miss Kovachev left, accompanied by her faithful maid, Mara. Mother said Great-aunt mustn't live alone anymore, and that's why she'd come to live with them. Great-aunt had been one of the most famous ballerinas of her day. She was the celebrated Laetitia Gavrilova, Mother said proudly. Nanny said Mara had been Great-aunt Laetitia's dresser throughout her career, and wherever Great-aunt had gone, Mara went, too. Great-aunt had danced in Monte Carlo, Leningrad, Moscow, Paris, Covent Garden in London—all over Europe—in fact, all over the world. That's what Nanny said, and Nettie couldn't wait to see her for she loved ballet, too—more than anything—and danced as much in her dreams as she did in the secrecy of her room, twirling around in her tutu which Mother had given her. Miss Kovachev had always been happy to take her to Covent Garden and Sadler's Wells Theatre. Perhaps now she could go with Great-aunt Laetitia.

So Nettie had been bursting with curiosity. She had never met a ballerina before; only seen them on stage, at a distance, looking so beautiful, so fairylike, so full of magic and enchantment that she often thought she would choke with her desire to be like them. She had been attending Miss Pollock's ballet classes since they arrived in London, but somehow, they stifled her imagination, and left her feeling frustrated.

On the day of Great-aunt's arrival, she had crept down to the second floor to spy. Great-aunt and Mara had been given an apartment on the second floor, which they would reach by the new lift. Mother had taken great pains to make it beautiful, putting in lovely furniture, Persian carpets, a grand piano set in the bay window, carefully chosen pictures by old masters, and, finally, her beloved mirrors to bring light into all the dark corners.

Nettie had peered eagerly through the banisters as pile upon pile of boxes and trunks were delivered and carried up to the apartment.

"I thought old people got rid of stuff at the end of their lives. Not this one!" muttered one of the maids. Then Nettie had seen Gimley, with a low bow, welcome a tiny, straight-backed old lady at the front door. She stood briefly in a pool of sunlight, looking frail and as shriveled as a leaf, as if with a puff of breath she could be blown away. Nettie had been appalled. *That can't be her. She's ancient!* Although she had been told that Great-aunt Laetitia was old, she couldn't believe anyone could be *this* old. How could Great-aunt have *ever* been a ballerina, ever been young? She was the oldest person Nettie had ever known, even though her hair wasn't white, but a dark red. "Dyed, of course," Nanny said later.

But that day had been memorable for more than the shock of seeing Great-aunt Laetitia. How could anyone forget? Her entry into the apartment had been accompanied by a long wailing scream, which sent everyone running to see what terrible accident had befallen her. There was the sound of splintering glass, of smashing and crashing, and Nettie flew to the scene in time to see frail Great-aunt, with amazing strength, flinging all Peachy's precious mirrors over the staircase and down onto the marble floors of the lobby. "No, no, no! That isn't me! Not meeeeee! Take them away!"

Her shrieks were interspersed with the softer, appealing tones of Mara, who spoke to her as if to a distressed child. "Hush, hush, Madame! We'll soon get rid of them." And she broke into angry French, glaring around at the bewildered staff. "*Comment a-t'il pu vous échapper qu'elle ne peut pas supporter les miroirs!* How could you not know that she can't stand mirrors!" she raged, then led her mistress away with soft murmurings. "*Ne vous inquiétez pas, chère Madame.* Don't upset yourself . . ."

Peachy came rushing up distraught and joined in the screams. "Oh, Auntie, what are you doing! My lovely mirrors! You didn't need to do that!"

"What's wrong?" Nettie had exclaimed hoarsely. "What's the matter?"

Even Vlad came bounding up the stairs two at a time, to see what had happened.

"Is she mad?" Nettie asked.

"No, dearest, not mad," soothed Nanny. "It's the mirrors. She can't bear mirrors."

"Mara should have warned us!" muttered Vlad angrily.

"Why, Daddy?" whispered Nettie wonderingly. "Why would Great-aunt do that?"

Still distressed, her mother put an arm around her. "I should have known. Oh dear, oh dear. My lovely mirrors! But it's my fault. I can't be angry with her. Come, I'll show you something." As a maid came scurrying with dustpan and brush to sweep up all the glass, she led Nettie to the library and sat her at the long mahogany table. Then she went to a shelf of albums, pulled out a big one, and set it before her. "Look!" She pointed. "Do you see? This is who your great-aunt was."

Nettie gazed upon a black-and-white photograph of a beautiful face. It looked a little like her mother, yet it wasn't. A young, *very* young woman stared out of the picture with eyes outlined like almonds; her cheekbones were high, her nose straight, her mouth soft, and her jawline lifted her chin up from her swanlike throat. Her hair was coiled back into the nape of her neck, giving her elegance and height. She looked like a girl waiting to go to a ball.

Mother sighed. "This is your great-aunt. When she was young, she was the most beautiful woman in the world, with her blue-green eyes, golden hair, and skin as fine as a peach. Her body was perfectly formed, and she moved like a fish darting upstream, or a bird soaring on the wind. She was painted and photographed by the finest in the world, and she was considered one of the most glorious ballet dancers of her time."

"She's like you, Mama. Your skin is as fine as a peach—that's why Daddy calls you Peachy," said Nettie, pressing her cheek against her mother's. She gazed in awe at picture after picture of a beautiful ballerina, in all kinds of poses, and all sorts of costumes, sometimes being lifted, whirled, or supported by a handsome prince. "I wish I could be like her—a ballerina. Miss Pollock says I'm the best in her class. I wish . . ." She trailed off dreamily. "Were you a dancer, too, Mama?"

Her mother kissed her, and held her close. "No. I can dance the tango and the salsa"—she laughed—"but not ballet! Anyway, I was married to your father by the time I was eighteen! Not like your great-aunt. She danced in public till she was over fifty! She could have married a hundred times over. Wherever she went, she was adored. Men worshipped her—princes, diplomats, millionaires, and generals all wanted to marry her—but she had vowed never to marry. 'I am wedded to my art!' she would say. Yet still, her admirers followed her around the world, attending all her performances, festooning her with flowers and presents. You'll see, even now, there are a few faithful ones left. They'll soon find out where she has gone to live, and we can expect bouquets of red roses to arrive at our door from time to time. Poor Aunt! Now she's just an old lady who can't bear to see herself old. Her body has withered, and yet her soul is that of a child, and her strength still extraordinary." Mother sighed. "All youth must fade. If only she could see that she has her own special beauty—beauty in her age."

How mysterious it all seemed to Nettie; how wonderful and yet, somehow, frightening. She glanced at her mother, who was beautiful and young. Nettie was sure that she never wanted to see her mother become like Great-aunt Laetitia. Nor did she want to think that she herself might look like that one day. After all, people were always telling Nettie how like her mother she was. She shuddered and jumped up. Ballerinas are always young. "I hate old people!" she muttered.

"No, Nettie! Don't say that. We all grow old."

But Nettie slipped away, leaving her mother still wistfully turning the pages.

At first, Nettie saw very little of Great-aunt Laetitia, who never joined them at the table for supper. Mara said her mistress preferred to eat in her own apartment, thank you very much, because she had very particular tastes. Sometimes she'd glimpse the two old ladies setting off on an excursion in the limousine, or clutching each other's arms as they entered the glass bubble elevator to go down to the gardens for their daily walk, or, if it was too cool, to sit in the conservatory. Where Great-aunt was as upright as an iron rod, and walked precisely, as if in time to music, with her feet turned out, Mara was a stooped, stocky old woman, with thin silver-white hair drawn back so fiercely into a bun that her scalp gleamed pink through the taut strands. Roly-poly-ish though she was, she moved like a mouse, creeping, sidling, suddenly scuttling at great speed, and called her mistress "Madame"—the French way—in an invariably respectful voice.

Leaning farther over the balustrade, Nettie stiffened with curiosity. There it was again, its image caught in a mirror below her—the same wavering fleeting reflection. It flitted past as swiftly as a wisp of cloud. Was it the Boy?

Immediately she fell into her own spying game. One night, Miss

Kovachev had caught her hiding behind a great, leafy philodendron watching one of her father's parties. She had knelt down beside her and whispered, "What are you doing?"

"Being a spy like James Bond," Nettie had whispered back with a giggle.

Miss Kovachev had ushered her back to bed and, as she tucked her in, asked seriously, "Have you a code name?"

Nettie shook her head. "No. What should it be?"

Miss Kovachev had thought deeply. "If James Bond is 007, then what about Star Spy .007? The decimal point is important," said Miss Kovachev. "It is the speck of stardust which makes you different, but as good as James Bond."

Nettie loved that. "Yes. I'll be Star Spy *Point* 007."

She had almost grown out of that game, but suddenly she wanted to play it again. Star Spy Point 007 dropped to her knees, crouching as if to avoid detection from an enemy. She sped down the staircase. Where was he? She crawled silently to the top of the staircase, her eyes spanning the entire atrium, just as Swivel-Eyes did. With her back to the banister, she eased her way down, step by step, her hand covering her imaginary pistol. She reached the next floor down, and leaped behind a pillar. With her back to it, she peered around to scan the corridor, and then sprang behind the large-leafed rubber plant. Again she looked everywhere, scrutinizing any spot where he might hide, waiting for him to make the first move. But there was nothing. She shuffled to the top of the next set of stairs down, did a mad dash, and landed up behind the potted aspidistra outside her great-aunt's door.

Piano music drifted out from Great-aunt's room. Nettie often heard it from her room above, and sometimes came out to sprawl along the landing on her tummy to listen.

The door was ajar, as if someone had forgotten to close it. Had the enemy gone inside? She had never entered her great-aunt's apartment before; never dared to. But this time she felt she could just peep.

Ready to draw out her imaginary gun, she peered inside to see a strange room. In the dim light, bare wooden floors stretched out before her. It was like an empty stage in a theatre, with heavy curtains looped by a velvet cord on either side of a bay window. In a far corner was a grand piano with a pair of candelabra burning. A dark silhouette hunched over the keys playing a waltz. The piano sounded hollow and distant. Shadows flickered, low lights glimmered and reflected in the bare oak floors as Nettie scanned around rapidly, always ready to flee. Where would he be? Was he hiding and peeping, just as she was, sneaking and creeping?

A rippling chord on the piano sounded as a ballerina in a soft white tutu sprang into the room. She pirouetted several times, posed in a deep arabesque, and sprang again, rising on her pointes. She was so slender, so tiny even; perfectly upright, head raised on a long neck, with one leg lifted up, as her body tipped down till her fingers touched the ground in front. She pattered gracefully around the room, her pointes making tiny squeaky thuds on the wooden floor. First she looked like a child, searching for something; then, as the pianist played flowing arpeggios, she moved her upper body as gracefully as a willow bending in the wind. The arpeggios got slower and slower, and she fluttered to the floor like a dying swan, tipping her face upwards as if to catch a last glimpse of a cloud-strewn sky. Her arms quivering, she stooped forwards to rest over an outstretched leg, her fingers curved over her satin foot. The last chords from the piano echoed emptily. Nettie was entranced. Who was she?

Although there were no mirrors, there were shimmering reflections. Nettie's shape reflected on the floor and in the highly polished cabinet doors. Without raising her head, the ballerina demanded in a high cracked voice, "Who's there, Mara? Is it that boy again?"

Nettie wanted to run, but she couldn't move. The dancer raised herself up and looked sightlessly into the gloom. With a sickening lurch in her stomach, Nettie saw this was not a child, nor a willow, but a very, very old Great-aunt Laetitia, with a powdered white face and lips as red as a smear of blood.

The terrible ballerina stood up, swaying slightly as if she were a strange puppet, dangling on strings. Everything about her was thin: her skin was so thin and translucent, it looked as if she was wrapped in the thinnest tissue paper. Beneath her white, feathery headdress, wisps of red hair fell upon her brow, making a shocking contrast with her paper-white forehead, through which Nettie felt she could almost look inside to her brain. Rising up on the tips of her ballet shoes, the creature pattered towards her with open arms, as if pleading; her skin stretched transparent over her thin hands, the blue veins running like narrow rivulets between her bony knuckles and tendons; thin, withered legs protruded from beneath her white, layered net tutu.

Nettie felt turned to stone. The piano stopped playing, and the ballerina halted, too. Old Mara scuttled out.

"Mara, is it that boy again?"

So there was a boy!

"No, Madame, it's Nettie."

"Nettie?" The voice sighed, as if trying to recall who Nettie was.

"Nettie, Madame. Peachy's child."

"Peachy's child? Ah, my little niece, Antonietta." Aged Great-aunt came off her pointes, looking even more like a bird with her turned-out silken feet. "Come here, child. Closer." Her eyes were vibrant, and gleaming with girlish energy; wide blue-green eyes—just as Mother had described—with eyebrows penciled into two thin curves almost as far as her temples. As she darted glances here and there, Nettie glimpsed the young girl in the photographs.

Nettie stepped forward as warily as Hansel and Gretel must have done when they met the witch in the Gingerbread House.

"Come, come, closer! Let me look at you. No, you're not that boy."

The ballerina sounded disappointed.

"Madame sees a boy."

"I do, too!" Nettie murmured.

"Maybe it's just shadows," suggested Mara.

"He's a naughty little imp, come from the other side. He moves things and sometimes steals," insisted Great-aunt, in a fierce whisper.

"Where's the other side?" Nettie whispered back.

"She means he's a ghost." Mara broke into a childish titter. "A naughty, naughty ghost—so mischievous. They can be like that sometimes—so restless! This little creature, I expect he lived here and, I suppose, died here—a bit of a handful, I daresay. He turns on taps and leaves the water running! Isn't that *très méchant*? So naughty! And he switches lights on and off, and puts things in the wrong drawers. When Madame's hairdresser came last week, the naughty boy hid her scissors. Oh, you should have seen the state she got into. Just grabbed her bag and ran, saying she'd never come here again. Mr. Barlow, the piano tuner, was also extremely upset because the wicked child messed up all his tuning forks. But do you know what?" Mara clasped Nettie's arm, and pulled her down so that her mouth was right into Nettie's ear. "He took my false teeth and hid them in the teapot. The doctor called by for tea. I took the lid off the pot to stir the tea and"—she broke into a high-pitched cackle—"do you know what? There were my teeth inside, grinning up at me. *Quel garçon! Quelle sottise!* Naughty boy! I scooped them out and popped them in my mouth. The doctor didn't think it was funny. Said he'd forgotten an appointment, and left without drinking his tea. Oh well! I don't suppose he'll be back either."

"Do you believe in ghosts? Do you, Mara?" Nettie was enthralled. Mara shrugged. "How should I know?"

"That's enough chitter chatter!" Great-aunt remonstrated. "You're worse than the boy. Let me see you, child!" Great-aunt jabbed a long, thin knobby finger to a spot in front of her.

Nettie flinched, and nearly cried *Don't touch me!* But Mara nudged her forward, even closer; close enough for Great-aunt to reach out and grasp her arm. Her touch was extraordinarily powerful, yet gentle, too. She released her arm but clasped Nettie's chin in the cup of her bony hand. She turned her head this way and then that, examining her profile. "Turn around," she ordered. Nettie turned. "Head up, shoulders back," she prodded her with the dreaded finger. Surprisingly, it tickled. Nettie wriggled and couldn't help a giggle escaping, even though she was still scared.

Mara cackled. "She's ticklish! Our little one is tickle ickle-icklish!"

"*Taisez-vous!* Quiet, woman!" snapped Great-aunt, and Mara put a hand across her mouth like a scolded little girl.

"Hmmm," pondered Great-aunt, still gripping her. "Your head sits well upon your shoulders, and your shoulders have a good shape; nicely sloping—an elegance even. Your spine is straight." She ran a finger down Nettie's back, causing her to wriggle and giggle again. "Hips—hmmm—they're strong, but not too broad—how old are you?"

"Twelve years and five months," replied Nettie.

"Already?" Great-aunt exclaimed in dismay. At first she frowned as she scrutinized Nettie. The girl looked more like nine, she was so small and slight. Then the frown vanished, and she smiled. "Hah! So, *ma petite!* Perhaps . . . But we have no time to lose. Take your shoes off and strip down to your knickers. Go on, go on! *Dépêche-toi!*" she urged as Nettie hesitated shyly.

"*Elle est belle!* She's going to be a beauty, this one; like you, Madame, and like her mother, too," cooed Mara, shuffling over to reassure Nettie. "You have the looks of a dancer, *mon enfant*, but now she wants to see whether you have the body."

"I have ballet lessons with Miss Pollock on Fridays," said Nettie as she jumped out of her jeans, her socks and sneakers. "I was top of my class."

"Bring a chair, Mara. Let her stand on it, so I can see her legs and feet," said Great-aunt, not responding to Nettie's piece of information.

"I was top of my class," repeated Nettie louder, thinking she might be deaf, but Great-aunt still made no response, stretching out her old woman's clawlike fingers to examine her legs and thighs, her feet and toes.

"Her legs are so long!" cooed Mara admiringly.

"Point your toes, one foot at a time," Great-aunt ordered. Nettie pointed into the palm of Great-aunt's hand; a pretty arch. She flexed each foot and rotated the ankles when told to.

"Do you like dancing?"

"I love it!" cried Nettie passionately. "Miss Kovachev used to take me to the ballet, but now she's gone, no one else has time. We saw

Swan Lake! It was beautiful. I wish I could be Odette." Odette was
the beautiful girl who was captured by an evil magician, and turned
into a swan.

"To be Odette, you would also have to be Odile," murmured
Great-aunt, and Nettie remembered that Odile was the evil magician's daughter, who through her father's magic looked exactly the
same as Odette. She and her father tricked the prince so that he
mistook Odile for Odette, and Odette, the girl he really loved, was
doomed to be a swan forever.

Great-aunt straightened with a rapid movement, and twirled away
girlishly. "Let's dance. Mara! *La musique!* Let's have Act One of
Swan Lake!"

Mara scuttled to the piano, and soon Tchaikovsky's ballet music
began to tinkle forth. Nettie leaped from the chair, and Great-aunt
glided into the center of the room, her arms waving gracefully. "It is
Prince Siegfried's birthday. There is a ball. All the girls want to
marry the handsome prince. Copy! Do as I do!" And Great-aunt
whirled away, transforming herself into a flirting young girl.

Nettie copied her, and for a while the two of them moved freely to
the rhythmic dance melodies, the rippling harplike sounds, the delicate trills.

"I can see why you were at the top of your class."

So she had heard.

"Come to me. I will teach you. You don't need anyone else when
you have the great Laetitia Gavrilova. Come every day, and I will
make a dancer of you. But you'll have to work. *Travailler!* Can you
work? Will you love it enough? Can you bear pain? *Il faut souffrir.*"

For the first time, Nettie looked into that old face; she glimpsed
the beauty it had once had. Her great-aunt's green eyes glittered
with intensity; her oval face, though riven with wrinkles under the

34

white makeup, still rose up from her long haggard neck, proud as a swan.

"Did you dance Odette/Odile?" Nettie asked with awe.

Aunt's head tipped into a perceptible, desperate "yes," as though she could hardly bear to remember those times past. "Will you come? Let me teach you?"

"Yes. Yes," said Nettie, and a strange shiver ran through her limbs.

"*La petite fille dit* yes! *Oui, oui, oui!*" Mara cackled with glee, as if somehow the child had brought some youth back to them.

"Come back tomorrow then," said Great-aunt.

Nettie put on her jeans and sat on the floor to pull on her socks and shoes. She saw the curtain twitch. A shadow flickered across the floor, the door moved slightly. Nettie looked up and caught Mara's gaze. Had she seen? She showed no sign.

"See you tomorrow!" cried Nettie, running out of the gloom into the mirror brightness of the corridor. She looked up and down, but there was no one to be seen. The corridor was empty.

There was a boy. I know there's a boy, but was he a ghost?

"Do you believe in ghosts?" Later, Nettie discussed it with Nanny George.

Nanny had always been in Nettie's life, as far back as she could remember, and Nettie couldn't imagine a time when she would no longer be there. Before any tutors came, it was Nanny who taught her to read and to count, Nanny who sang her nursery rhymes and read her bedtime stories, and Nanny who was there from first thing in the morning to last thing at night. And apart from her regular two-week holiday twice a year, Nanny had been there virtually every day of her life. It was to Nanny George that Nettie always went first when she had anything to tell, and when Nettie asked her if she believed in ghosts, Nanny's round blue eyes widened with disapproval. "Certainly not," she pronounced categorically.

"Mara says there's a ghost in their apartment." Nettie ignored Nanny's look. "He's naughty. He moves things about, and leaves faucets running, and do you know what he did with Aunt Mara's false teeth?" Nettie giggled with glee. "He put them in the teapot! Mara says he comes from the other side. Where's the other side?"

"Hmmm!" grunted Nanny. "Some people think you can talk to the dead on the other side of life, but in my opinion, there's usually a rational explanation," she said calmly. "You get forgetful when you're old, and even when you're not old. You move things; forget where you've put them. With those two old creatures, I expect they move each other's things all the time and, by way of an excuse, blame a 'ghost.' "

But I've seen a . . . Nettie was going to say but, seeing Nanny's blue eyes cloud with disapproval, told her instead how, from now on, Great-aunt Laetitia was going to teach her ballet.

A finger had trailed through the dust gathered on the shiny wooden banister. A maid noticed it as she polished, and hoped it wasn't Mrs. Roberts, who was such a stickler and demanded high standards. But then, no, she decided. It couldn't be Mrs. Roberts. She would never have done more than swipe a finger across the surface and call for the housekeeper. This trailing finger had gone down two floors, and stopped.

Everyone noticed the change in Nettie. She had stopped mooning around and was full of gaiety and excitement. When Peachy wanted Nettie to go to Paris with her for some shopping, Nettie said, "Oh

no, Mama! I've got to practice. I've got a ballet lesson coming up
with Great-aunt," and Peachy had hugged her fondly, relieved that
she had at last begun to forget Miss Kovachev. She smiled to see
Nettie enthusiastic again, something she'd never really been with
poor Miss Pollock, and sent a message to say Nettie would no
longer be coming for lessons.

At the time arranged, Nettie put on her pale pink leotard and
scuttled downstairs to Great-aunt's apartment for her second lesson. She slipped off her sandals and tied on her pink leather ballet
shoes. She could hear the piano playing. With a shiver of expectation, she slipped inside. There in the low lighting was Great-aunt,
dressed in a black practice skirt, with pink tights and pink ballet
shoes. In her hand, she held a long, silver-topped cane.

"We have to turn you out; feet out, knees out, thighs out. We will
go through your basic positions today," announced Great-aunt.
"Show me your first position."

Nettie screwed up her nose. "I know those. I learned them years
ago."

"Pah!" snorted Great-aunt. "Teachers these days don't know how
to teach. I have to be sure you haven't picked up any bad habits, so
I will start from the beginning. You will just do what I ask, child."

From her place at the piano, Mara waved with fluttering fingers,
and blew her an encouraging kiss. Nettie gave a quick wave back,
then dutifully stood upright in first position. As she went through
her basic positions, Great-aunt screeched at her like a wild bird.
"Out, out! Turn those knees *out*! And your feet—*mon Dieu!* You are
rrrolling over!" She rolled her *r*s as the French do, and rapped Nettie's ankles with her cane. "Balance your weight on both feet! Hold
your body up, as if you are being pulled upwards; as if you might lift
off the ground. Up, up!" The cane came under her chin. "Head

up!" With every command, Great-aunt's cane prodded and tapped.

For nearly an hour, Nettie toiled through her standing positions, in time to Mara's exercise music, and was just beginning to think her muscles wouldn't perform another task when Great-aunt waved her stick in the air and cried, "*Ça suffit!* Enough! Enough of that! Let's dance! Mara—music! A waltz!" Mara went into a lilting waltz, and Great-aunt transformed into a joyful young girl at her first dance, whirling gracefully around the room. "Come on! Dance! Feel the rhythm!" She clasped Nettie's hands. And so Nettie danced and, with a surge of surprise as if she had never really thought it before, she exclaimed inside her head, *When I grow up I want to be a dancer!*

After the lesson, Great-aunt taught her to say "thank you" with a deep curtsy, the ballet way, and Nettie kissed her goodbye on both cheeks, the French way, and danced off to find her shoes. But they had gone. She searched everywhere.

"It's that naughty boy. I told you. Didn't I? Didn't I?" shrieked Mara.

"Yes, Mara." Great-aunt sighed. "But he does no harm." And Nettie realized that even though the boy was naughty, Great-aunt was fond of him.

"No, you're right. He does no harm," agreed Mara, and tittered affectionately.

"But where are my shoes?" cried Nettie.

"I expect they'll turn up. They usually do. The boy's not a thief. Don't worry about it. I'm sure you've another pair you can wear in the meantime," said Mara, trying to make light of it.

So Nettie returned to the third floor in her ballet shoes. But when she reached her own door, there neatly placed outside were her shoes.

"How did they get there?" she marveled. "Perhaps there is a ghost!"

"Really, Nettie. Get such a thought out of your head," said Nanny, who was tidying her room. "I cannot encourage you to believe in ghosts and fairies and superstition. They're just two old ladies, living in their fantasies. A maid must have brought them to your door. Ask the doorman to check the security cameras. You see! Ella probably brought them while you were having your lesson, or even Mara herself."

It couldn't have been Mara, thought Nettie, perplexed. *She was playing the piano.*

"Their brains are full of stories from the ballet. They act them out, and forget what reality really is," declared Nanny. "And as for ghosts! No more of that nonsense, Nettie. It's naughty of your great-aunt to put such ideas into your head."

Nettie wondered what Miss Kovachev would have thought. What a shame she had left before Great-aunt Laetitia and Mara came. Miss Kovachev had never talked about ghosts, and Nettie didn't even know if she believed in them. She sighed. Now she couldn't ask her.

Somehow, Nettie was drawn back to Miss Kovachev's room in the Round Tower. She opened the door, slipped inside, and closed it behind her. Her heart was thumping—as if she was doing wrong, taking a risk, holding a deadly secret. There was a soft green stillness. Everything looked the same, yet there was the emptiness of an unoccupied room, the feeling of absence.

From the window, clouds dusted across the sky over the city, as if swept by a broom, coiling up at the edges in soft wisps. She didn't know what it was that suddenly tingled up her spine, as if Great-aunt Laetitia had walked her fingers up her vertebrae, one by one; a strong sense of not being alone; of someone else being present. A strange rosy light filled the room like sunlight filtering through water; the bed seemed to float. Nettie lay down on the round bed, stretching out her limbs, merging into the imprint she imagined her former tutor's body had left. *I will be Odette, the white swan who Prince Siegfried loved. I will fly over the city and find you.* But what about Odile, Odile the evil magician's daughter who, Nettie remembered, wore a black tutu? Am I her too?

With half-closed eyes, she gazed up at the ceiling. The light and shadows filtered through the curtains across the ceiling, creating pictures. She saw faces and bodies, a mysterious lake surrounded by trees, and white swans flying in with singing, zinging wings spreading out as they came in to land. Emerging through the pictures, the light also fell on squiggles in the plaster, looking almost like words. She felt as if the room was full of messages—that it was trying to tell her something. Her fingers fell over the side of the bed and, lifting the quilt, she mindlessly trailed them along the wooden frame, normally hidden by a valance. She paused, feeling something in the wood under her fingers: a join. She rubbed it, then rolled over onto her tummy to see what it was. Her fingers had discovered a drawer which had been fitted under the bed for extra storage space. Taking hold of the small brass ring, she pulled. The drawer opened smoothly. It was empty except . . . she just glimpsed something pushed to the back, as if deliberately hidden. Briefly her fingers touched silk—a scarf perhaps—when a soft tapping startled her.

Thrusting the drawer shut, she rolled off the bed and hurriedly straightened it. Guilt overwhelmed her as if she'd been caught prying or stealing. Any moment she expected the bedroom door to open. But who would walk in? Miss Kovachev? Her heart beat fiercely. But the door didn't open, and no one came in.

The tapping continued. It wasn't from the bedroom, but—the bathroom! It was coming from the bathroom. Tentatively, Nettie tiptoed across the room and peered inside. It was just as she had last seen it: a small, round room of pure white tiles, with a rounded bath fitted like a semicircle into the round walls, a washbasin, a shower, a cabinet, and a broom cupboard. She opened the cabinet. It was empty; no forgotten toothbrush, or even a half-squeezed tube of toothpaste, no paper tissues, spare soap, or that bottle of eau de cologne—the only perfume Miss Kovachev had ever used.

A further sharp tap made her jump nervously. It came from behind her.

"Nettie, Nettie!" a chill voice breathed from inside the broom cupboard.

With a gasp of terror, Nettie fled; fled from the bathroom, fled from the Round Tower, down the steps and to her living room, where she slammed the door shut and flung herself into the corner of the sofa, her heart thumping fit to jump from her body.

4

SOMETHING LEFT BEHIND

Miss Kovachev had left something. Nettie knew she must go back and look in the drawer under the bed. Yet there was something in this house; something which moved things, and seemed able to roam around the house; something which might have been watching her in the round room—perhaps was watching her now. Was there really a ghost? Was it the boy?

Suddenly, there were footsteps, a sharp knock, and the door flew open. Her mother, Peachy, burst into her room dressed for riding in jodhpurs, white shirt, and riding boots. "Sweetie! Daddy wants us all to go riding before supper. Now don't say you've got ballet practice. I know you've had your lesson. He's been away such a lot, and is longing for quality time with his darling daughter. Get changed quickly. It's a lovely afternoon."

But Nettie stayed curled up tightly on the sofa, her knees drawn up to her chin, her eyes staring fearfully at the door.

"Are you feeling all right?"

Nettie uncoiled and flung her arms around her mother. "Do you believe in ghosts?"

"Of course not! Have you been having bad dreams? Come on. Daddy's waiting."

Ella arrived to help her on with her jodhpurs and boots, and she joined her mother at the mews door, as Peckham, their chauffeur, arrived with the limousine. Sitting alongside him was Hepworth, another bodyguard. Nettie and her mother slid into the back. Swivel-Eyes was already astride his motorbike, and followed them, turning out onto the busy road heading for the park. When they reached the stables at the far end of the park, he carried on past as if he had nothing to do with them.

Ethan, Nettie's father's personal bodyguard, was already there, dressed for riding, adjusting his saddle, but watching, always watching. He never rode alongside them, but a few paces behind, though sometimes he galloped on ahead, then waited for them to pass him. There had always been an Ethan in her life; and a Hepworth and a Swivel-Eyes. It's what people had, so thought Nettie, along with butlers, valets, maids, chauffeurs, and cooks. She never questioned their role. She knew not to greet the bodyguards in public. It was as if they were invisible, and the casual eye would not have linked Ethan to mother and daughter taking their evening ride around the park.

"Where's Daddy?" asked Nettie as the groom gave her a leg up onto her pony.

"He'll be along soon. Just had a couple of calls to make first," said Mother reassuringly, though Nettie knew how rarely her father had time to join them—even when he promised—and how often their time together would be interrupted by a phone call or a sudden appointment.

As the afternoon deepened into evening, golden light trickled through the branches of the maple trees that lined the riding track. It gleamed in the rich chestnut of the horses' bodies, their tails flaring like comets. It outlined their twitching ears and flowing manes.

Nettie felt most at peace when she was riding, though this was one activity she had never shared with Miss Kovachev. It was her own special time with her mother; a precious time when they were more like equal friends, rather than mother and child.

They had ridden halfway around the track, and were passing some plane trees with their broad mottled trunks and great swooping boughs, when a shaft of light fell, catching the figure of a young woman. She was walking down the avenue toward the wrought-iron gates of the park. "Miss Kovachev! Mama, that's Miss Kovachev, isn't it?" Nettie squealed, standing up in her stirrups. The woman was wearing the same sort of dark clothes, and the head scarf that Miss Kovachev always wore when she went out.

"Can't be, darling. She's gone to Bulgaria, supposedly to look after her sick father. Are you ready for a gallop? Come on!" And she dug her heels into the horse's sides and broke into a canter.

"Miss Kovachev!" Nettie's voice rang high and clear through the breezeless air. She swore the woman hesitated, but she didn't look back, and then walked even faster. "Look around, please look around," Nettie prayed under her breath. "Miss Kovachev—it's me, Nettie!" But the woman hurried through the gates and vanished into a cluster of people making for the underground.

"It was her, it was her. Mama! Stop her!" Nettie broke into a desperate gallop to catch up with her mother. "That was Miss Kovachev, wasn't it? Why did you say she'd gone to Bulgaria? You told me you didn't know where she'd gone. I want her to come back. Why can't she? Why does everyone keep things from me? I hate you all." All Nettie's pent-up bewilderment and grief poured out as she raged at her mother.

There was a shocked silence. Nettie had never spoken like that to her mother before.

"We, er . . . only heard the other day that she'd gone back home. I forgot to say anything," her mother faltered. "Oh, do forget her. Come on—I'll race you to the back gate."

She's lying! thought Nettie in disbelief. Mothers don't lie, surely? She felt a strange and sudden void open up inside her. If she had lied about that, what else would she lie about? At a stroke, the world seemed a different place.

The golden dust in the shafts of light reminded her of stardust. Everything seemed to break up into shimmering atoms; even the thoughts in her head, the feelings inside her, the sounds all around her: voices, laughter, and traffic, all danced with meaning yet without any meaning she could understand. She was a child yet not a child. Peachy diminished as though through the wrong end of a telescope, breaking up into particles and merging with the sunbeams. Nettie's horse, sensing her distracted control, broke into a canter, his hooves thudding the ground. The atoms merged once more, back into their component parts, and the world swung back into focus. She saw dogs chasing, and a group of schoolchildren in very bright blue blazers. They were laughing and joking and fooling about, and she wished she could have been among them, too.

At the bend of the track, also coming into focus in the dappled light, was Ethan—and there was her father, mounted on his shining black horse, ambling towards them talking on his cell phone. Peachy had just galloped up to him, blowing him kisses.

"Hey, Nettie, my little cherub! You're a pretty good rider now." Vlad smiled, ending the call and slipping the phone into his pocket. "Mama thinks you should enter a gymkhana this summer, but I think we're going to have to buy you another horse. You're growing so fast. Soon you won't be my little cherub." He puffed a kiss to her across his palm. "You're turning into an angel, and we'll have to keep up with you, especially if my angel wants to be a champion horsewoman. I want you to go to Frithwood and check out a horse I asked Uncle Kory to get you. Can you go on Saturday morning? It's a handsome young gelding. It could be just the one for you."

Frithwood was their country house, where they bred racehorses. Usually Nettie loved going there, but this time she said, "Oh! I can't go on Saturday, I have a ballet lesson with Great-aunt."

"Really, darling!" exclaimed Mama. "You've only just had one."

Vlad drew alongside. "What's this I hear? You prefer a ballet lesson to buying a new horse? Mama did say you were visiting Great-aunt quite often."

"Old people love visits," agreed Peachy, "and it's very kind of you, Nettie, but I'm sure she'll understand if you don't go for once. You can make it up another time. Now that I've persuaded Daddy that you need a good competition horse, I don't want to waste time. You won't win those ribbons with Firecracker."

"I don't visit her to be *kind*," protested Nettie, avoiding looking at her mother. "I do love riding. I love my horse, but . . ." She faltered, because she'd never quite thought of it before in the same way. "I love ballet even more. Great-aunt thinks I'm good. She says I have the body of a dancer, and . . . I love it, much more than I did with Miss Pollock. I love riding, too, Daddy, I really do, but not as much now."

"Poor Miss Pollock. Weren't you her star pupil? You're such a talented girl," Vlad cooed fondly. "Dance all you want, sweetie, but don't give up riding. Uncle Kory thinks he's found you a perfect pony."

"Come and watch me dance with Great-aunt! Will you?" Nettie looked appealingly at her father. How she wished she could see more of him. But he was always busy—either with Mama, playing golf at the club, or flying his own jet off on business trips. When she did see him, he was so kind. He whirled her up, hugged and kissed her, and called her his princess. And he always came back from a trip abroad with a present.

"I tell you what!" said her father. "I'm off to Russia in a few days and very busy till then. I'll watch you when I'm back. But go and see this pony at Frithwood. Uncle Kory's expecting you. Dancing needn't be a reason not to have a good horse."

All three of them broke into a trot, riding side by side. "Like the Three Musketeers!" Vlad laughed. Then his phone went off again.

Nettie waited patiently till his conversation was over, and said, "Daddy! I'm sure I saw Miss Kovachev. Mama said she'd gone to look after her father, but if she did, she's back. Why can't she teach me again? I don't like Don. He's boring. Please. I could write and ask her, couldn't I, if you have her address? Do you?" pleaded Nettie.

Her mother and father exchanged glances across her.

"Darling, I told you, you were wrong," insisted Mother. "Miss Kovachev's gone now. We don't know where she is; took off, just like that, without any notice. Some of these girls, they flit out of your life without so much as a note. Of course she can't come back. I wouldn't have her. Not after leaving us in the lurch." Her voice was suddenly hard.

"But you said she'd gone to Bulgaria!" Nettie challenged her accusingly.

"I only heard that from one of the maids later. She could at least have had the decency to send us a note—but there was nothing.

Darling, why are you making such a fuss? You've never cared before about who came and went. Please forget it," Mother said abruptly.

"Daddy?" Nettie entreated her father to take her side. For a moment, his face looked oddly cold. His eyes stared ahead, slightly narrowed. Then he blinked rapidly, as she sometimes saw him do after he'd been thinking, and he stuck his heels into his horse's flanks. "Don's your tutor now, and I hope you'll take your lessons seriously with him. Come on! I'll race you!" And Vlad galloped off ahead of them, followed by Peachy, crouched over her saddle as she hurtled after him.

"I hate Don," Nettie murmured into thin air. She glanced around the park, wishing she could glimpse Miss Kovachev once more, then nudged her pony forward. She was sure there was something her mother and father weren't telling her.

That night, Nettie couldn't sleep. In her dreams, she rode a black horse across a starry sky. "There's Jupiter, and Venus!" She heard Miss Kovachev's voice. She was standing on a star, pointing. "And look! That shining planet is Earth. That's where we live."

Nettie was so pleased to see her. "Why did you go? Why didn't you tell me, or say goodbye?" But then Miss Kovachev seemed to be floating away, and no matter how hard Nettie urged on her black horse, digging her heels into its flanks, she couldn't catch up with her.

"Save me, save me!" Miss Kovachev's arms reached out desperately, as she floated away until she was just a tiny speck, and soon the clouds rolled across the sky and she vanished.

Nettie woke up with a start. Tears were running down her face. Strangely, she hadn't dreamed about Miss Kovachev since she left. Yet she couldn't help feeling there was something wrong; something wrong about the way she had left; something wrong about the way no one talked about her at all.

Perhaps Miss Kovachev was dead. Perhaps she'd seen a ghost of Miss Kovachev in the park. Perhaps the ghost in Great-aunt's apartment wasn't a boy, but Miss Kovachev.

Nettie was wide awake now, and her fear replaced by determination. She must be as brave as Point 007. If Miss Kovachev was a ghost, then she had nothing to fear. She was her friend. She would go back to the Round Tower. She would look inside that drawer under the bed, and find the one thing Miss Kovachev had left behind.

Without putting on the light, Nettie slipped into the corridor. As always, it was swathed in a soft night-light. When she reached the Round Tower, she opened the door quietly and slipped into the hazy darkness inside.

She paused and began to shiver, not with cold, but with nervous expectation. A bright moon pierced through the slitted windows. She had no need of extra light. Everything was visible in the pale gloom. She glided towards the bed, almost wondering whether she might see Miss Kovachev lying there, her eyes open, as bright as stars. But the bed was as it had been before, a little rumpled from where Nettie herself had lain. She crouched on the floor, pulled open the drawer, and reached inside.

She had to extend her full arm before her fingers touched something—the silky scarf. Was that all Miss Kovachev had left? She pulled it towards her, but it resisted. There was something else. She tugged harder, and something solid came into her grasp. She lifted it out, and without unwrapping it put her face to the scarf and breathed in. It smelled of eau de cologne, Miss Kovachev's smell. Slowly, she unwrapped it and revealed a notebook. She put on the bedside light. Her hand trembled as she opened it. It was written by hand, in ink and pencil. She flicked through a few pages and groaned with disappointment. It wasn't in English; she couldn't even understand more than a few letters from the alphabet, the script was so strange. She turned a few more pages, then, among all the incomprehensible squiggles, she saw six letters she could read: *Nettie.*

Me. My name. She's writing about me. She turned the page; it was densely written in this strange script. She almost missed another sentence in English, buried in the gobbledygook.

I want her to know. Oh God! How can I tell her?

Does she mean me? What should I know? Nettie fumbled through, page after page, looking for her name again. Miss Kovachev had wanted to tell her something, but what?

She lay back on the bed and pulled the coverlet over her. She held the book to her chest, as if somehow it would translate itself . . .

Nettie . . . dear Nettie, I want you to know about me, but how can I bring myself to tell you? In knowing about me, you will have to learn more about yourself which you may not like—which may destroy you . . .

5

The Notebook Speaks

I must write this down. I want you to know the truth . . .

The words struggled to be heard inside the closed pages of the notebook. They had the life and breath of their author—the desperate hand that wrote them, the tears that sometimes blotted the pages, the searing thoughts and feelings.

I am writing this down because I can't understand what happened. I can't tell anyone—for there is no one who speaks my language—and no one who would understand, anyway. It's as though, by leaving my home and my own country, I have stepped into another universe—where hardly anything makes sense. Yes—there is land, sea, and sky. I feel the earth beneath my feet, the heavens above my head. There is night and day, hot and cold, wet and dry, and I think there is sleeping and waking, conscious and unconscious—but now I flounder; I am not sure. I seem to have lost sense of reality. I think back to the night I arrived in this country, a night brittle with frost, when diamond-hard constellations studded a leather-black sky.

We had been driving for weeks across Europe, to be dumped, finally, on the other side of the English Channel and abandoned. I had felt so afraid. Well, I couldn't remember a day in the last six months when I hadn't felt a long, dull, aching fear. But somehow this was different. This was a fierce, present, of-the-moment, scalding terror. Everyone must have felt the same, because as if by instinct, my fellow travelers vanished; hurriedly dispersing for fear of being seen by the authorities. It was each one for themselves.

I knew how conspicuous I must look—a woman alone in my long skirt, shabby raincoat, and head scarf; everything around me—the trees, the fields, the road, the lampposts—were all screaming "foreigner, illegal, lost," and I, too, fled into the shadows, huddling into myself until I found the courage to set off. I knew only one thing—that I must find my way to London. That's where Anna was.

I ate an apple which I'd stored in my pocket. I was starving, and I chewed it right down—core and all. It gave me the strength to finally set off towards London, walking while it was still night to avoid detection.

How my legs ached. I was hardly able to lift one foot up after another as I trudged on and on in the pitch black, with only the palest moonlight glistening on the frost. I kept away from main roads, following tracks alongside hedgerows, furtive as the fox whose eyes gleamed at me out of the darkness. I was hungry—oh so hungry—and getting colder all the time. A hopeless fatigue dragged at my limbs. I only wanted to curl up into a hedge and sleep, just sleep. I didn't care if it meant death.

Then my feet struck the hard tarmac. It jolted me awake. I was on the road again. A huge sign loomed before me glinting its information: LONDON 65 MILES. I despaired. Sixty-five miles! I won't make it! Then I saw them: two blazing lights like comets entering the atmosphere, appearing out of the darkness. Hide! I must hide. But my legs were rooted. It was a car speeding towards me. I froze as the beams swept over me and caught me like a wild animal in their spotlight. The car braked violently to a stop.

I tried to back away; back into the wild fields beyond the hedges. It might be the police. What if it was the police? They'd send me all the way back. I couldn't bear that.

A shadowy man leaned sideways and opened the passenger door. The interior car light came on, but I couldn't make out his features. He called out in English, "You okay?"

I was too terrified to open my mouth. He would know I was a foreigner. I nodded stupidly. "Okay, thanks," and strode on, trying to look as if I knew where I was going.

"Want a lift?" The car cruised after me, the door still held open.

Danger! My brain was shouting, "No, no, no!" But my body was weakly beseeching, "Yes, yes, yes!" I stumbled, my legs almost giving way.

"Nina? It's you, isn't it? Come on, get in. I'll give you a lift."

I was stupefied. He called my name. He spoke my language. He knew me. I turned with joy—it didn't seem possible, yet it seemed like an answer to a prayer.

"Who are you?" I limped closer, trying to see his face—but somehow, it was in shadow.

He just patted the passenger seat and said reassuringly, "You look all done in. Come, let's get going."

I got in, though my brain still clamored, "Don't, don't, don't!"

He pulled the door shut, and the light went off. "Buckle up!"

I fumbled with the seat belt. He helped me, then pulled away with a screech of tires. "So how's the family, Nina? They got your father, didn't they? Bad. Your brothers, too—all but little Leon—poor kid. It's a lousy world. He must miss you. So must your younger sister, poor little Katya!"

He drove fast. I stared at the road ahead gleaming like the back of a snake. The headlights strafed the rigid fields on either side, empty, silent, white in the moonlight, and all the while, he talked and talked all about me. I tried to ask him who he was, but I couldn't. It was like being in a nightmare. After the freezing cold outside, the warmth inside the car was almost suffocating. All I wanted to do was surrender to the deep comfortable passenger seat. Yet I couldn't, I kept myself upright, as rigid as the frost-stiffened landscape, sitting forward, alert with anxiety, thinking I should be prepared to throw myself from the car. I wanted to look at the face of this man who had just picked me up, but I didn't dare. Who would I see? Somehow it terrified me more than not knowing. I didn't know if he was real even. In that dark, alien night, I felt as though I had stepped into another time zone; another dimension. He knew me, but how?

"And what about the other one; Anna, isn't it? No news from her, eh? Fancy her disappearing like that. Girls these days . . . !"

"Anna!" I cried out. He mentioned Anna, my darling older sister, who had gone into the city to a job, and never been seen again. "Do you know where she is? Is she in London or Copenhagen?"

It was as though he hadn't heard me; he just went on talking and talking . . . "But children are adaptable—thank God! Good thing, otherwise the world would be even worse than it is. Is your mother coping? Fell apart after your father was killed, so I hear," he continued, his voice concerned and warm with friendly interest, as if we were sitting around the iron stove back home, sipping peach brandy and chewing on hot crispy fatted bacon. "I hope she's not having trouble with that back of hers. Bad luck, eh, what with all the other disasters? But she's a good woman—that mother of yours. Oh yes. Brave, too. If anyone can get by, she will. She'll have prepared the goose for

Christmas dinner, eh? That good neighbor, Trikov, will have given her one, that's for sure. They'll be at midnight mass now. Pity you're not there. Katya and your mother, they'll be lighting a candle for you and Anna, crying for you both."

I tried to open my mouth; ask again, "Who are you?" but the words couldn't come out, and on he talked, on and on . . . till my head swam with weariness. *Who are you, who are you?* But it was as if I was struck dumb. I didn't dare to ask the question in case the answer was too terrible.

A stranger had come out of an alien night in this alien country, as arbitrary as a shooting star; as random a meeting as any that could be envisaged, yet it was as if we had met by design, at a prearranged rendezvous.

He spoke as if he were from my village; as if he had been there when they came for my father and brothers; seen them bundled into the back of a truck, while Katya, my little sister, was howling with panic, screaming for someone to stop them. He spoke as if he had seen my mother trying to clamber on board the truck, too, when it had pulled away so fast she had fallen, screaming with pain and despair. He knew that Anna had gone to the city looking for work, and then disappeared, and that months later, a single letter came from Copenhagen. I read it, because my mother couldn't read. Anna was working there, but said she had been offered a marvelous job in London. She didn't say what. She said she loved us. That was two years ago, and no one heard from her again. Mother was frantic. But we were too poor, living in too much terror to go and look for her. And where would she have gone? I had heard of other girls vanishing like Anna; rumors abounded; that she was forced into crime, that she was working in a sweatshop, that she had been bought and sold like a slave. "She could be anywhere; London, Hamburg, Bangkok—anywhere. Best to stop thinking about it," people told us. "Think of her as dead. You'll never see her again."

My throat and mouth were dry with fear. He must be one of them; one of the Mafia; or perhaps the secret police. He must have followed me all that way. Perhaps he had already killed Kusa. Now he had captured me. Where would he take me? What would he do to me? Would he torture me first? Oh God, no! Not torture. I couldn't bear pain. I've seen them; people from my village who resisted the gangs and had been tortured, returning to the village, their bodies broken, their spirit destroyed. No, no, I couldn't bear that.

"So, Nina! What about you?" The voice flowed on like syrup. "Still want to be a teacher, eh? You were hoping to get out of the village, eh? No goose girl you! Hoping you could go to university? What about that book you always wanted to write? Perhaps you'll get to do it now that you're out of that mess. Though I never understand how writers can go into exile, away from their own language and culture."

I nodded mechanically, and tried again to speak, but he carried on, talking. "How are your cousins, Dragna and Boris . . . ?" He listed all the members of my family by name, asking after each one, yet not giving me a spare second for a reply. "Pity about the troubles. Bad luck about what happened to you, being thrown out of your home like that. But that landlord of yours—Robart—he knew how to wheedle his way into your mother's affections, eh! Trying to get yours, too? It's a bad world for a fatherless girl—and Uncle Tony! No help at all, eh? Pah! You could have done without that—having to leave home. I just hope you will manage without Kusa."

He knew everything. Oh God! *Who was this man?* How did he know about that monster, Robart, or that I'd quarreled with my uncle at home and been thrown out? How did he know about Kusa?

"Stop the car! Please stop, I'm going to be sick." I was retching now, trying to swallow the bile rising up my gullet.

He pulled over without a word, while I flung open the door and, still held by my seat belt, leaned out and vomited. He flipped a white handkerchief out of his breast pocket and chucked it onto my lap. "Here, wipe your mouth with this." When I was done, he pressed the accelerator and moved back onto the road. I lurched with the motion, slamming shut the door.

I leaned back in my seat and closed my eyes. The perspiration beaded on my brow. At last I heard my voice coming from somewhere deep within me. "Do you know where Kusa is?"

"No." The single syllable died in the darkness.

6

BACK STAIRS

The next day, Nettie's parents were holding a lunch party. They were always holding parties; cocktail parties, Christmas parties, costume parties, birthday parties; any excuse for a party—they loved them. "It oils the wheels," said her father, and the whole household would scurry around bringing in huge bundles of fresh flowers flown in from Thailand or Africa, crates of wine and champagne from their own vineyards in Spain and France. Vans full of provisions from Fortnum and Mason and Harrods rolled up to the service entrance early that morning, and soon the chefs and kitchen staff set about producing incredible dishes: stuffed dumplings, scales of cucumber adorning huge platters of salmon, meat and game, roast vegetables and vast bowls of salad, quiches and pastries, and cheeses flown in from Italy and Switzerland. Peachy prided herself on her kitchen, and their guests knew that they would get the finest food in London.

How beautiful Peachy looked, as she greeted her guests in her latest designer dress, a low-cut pale peach silk sheath, which clung to her slim body, her white long neck, and willow-like arms. And there was Vlad, looking so elegant in a flamboyant bottle green velvet jacket. Although he wasn't tall, his body was broad and muscular;

his presence was like a prowling lion. People admired him, flattered him, talked to him, yet kept a respectful distance, and made way for him as if, perhaps, they also feared him.

Nettie had never feared her father. She rushed up for a hug, and he stroked her hair while continuing a conversation with a pale, narrow-faced man, with mobile eyes which never quite caught hers.

"Nigel, meet my daughter. Sweetie, this is Mr. Raycroft. He's a lawyer; the kind of man we hope to have on our side if ever we get into trouble! Isn't that so, Nigel?" And her father roared with laughter.

Nettie knew that so many of her father's friends were "important," like high court judges, police inspectors, members of parliament, titled people, bishops, and "people in high places," but she hated the way they talked down to her, or patted her as if she were a household pet while all the time carrying on a conversation with her father. She wandered away amid the swish of satin and silk, the clink of champagne glasses, and the air layered with cigar smoke and perfume.

"You okay, poppet?" asked her mother, noting her daughter's gloomy face. Like a mermaid, she glided towards her through the throng, jewels glistening on her skin like drops of water. "You're not catching a cold or something?"

"No. I'm—"

"Oh, sweetie, there's Uncle Charlie. I must get him a drink." With an almost aquatic movement, Peachy dived away from her daughter, calling over her shoulder, "Do try not to look so bored. Pleeeease. See you in a minute."

Nettie wasn't sure what word she would use to describe how she felt. Not "bored." She was hardly ever bored. It was a thought nagging inside her—thoughts about the notebook.

She wandered out into the conservatory, which had been added to the house when they moved in. Nettie had grumbled that the new house had no swimming pool and, before she knew it, the builders were there and created a marvelous one in the back garden.

After changing into her bathing suit, she wandered among the marble pillars and statues entwined with flowering creepers. There was a steamy warmth layered with rich smells from palms, and banana trees; from the mimosa, acacia, gardenia, and magnolia which lined the curving edge of the swimming pool. An arched ceiling of golden mosaic gleamed overhead like a sky at dawn, while below the surface of the water, the sides and floor were of darkest blue Moroccan tiles, so that Nettie felt she dived into an inky night.

She swam hard, racing up and down. It wasn't that she felt ill, as her mother had surmised, at least not ill in body, but somehow deep in her soul she felt ill at ease. For the first time in her life she felt lonely. Her whole world was with her parents and their friends, and it had never occurred to her before to feel lonely. Throughout her life, they had given her everything she ever needed, but something had changed, and today she felt hollow inside—a strange emptiness. If only she could read that notebook. It seemed to be calling to her: "Read me, read me." Understand.

I tried to tell my mother what Robart, our landlord, was doing to me. But she couldn't believe it; wouldn't. She said I was lying, and sided with that man. She even told him what I had accused him of. He beat me up and told me to get out. Leave the village. Of course, Mother repented, and begged him to let me stay, she fell at his feet and wept. "She's only sixteen. What will become of her?" But I wouldn't have stayed anyway. I would have run away. I would go to

London and look for Anna, and if I couldn't find her, I'd look after myself; anything to get away from Robart.

Uncle Tony saw me onto a bus, shuffling, and embarrassed, he paid for my ticket, and walked away before the bus even left.

It was night when the bus reached the city. The passengers straggled out into a blast of cold air, hardly speaking. They were mostly peasants, with their beans-and-potatoes-sturdy figures, waddling rhythmically along, weighed down by their bags and suitcases. They all seemed to know where they were going, and had soon disappeared. I felt conspicuous, standing alone and uncertain. It was a hateful place. A rat scuttled along the edge of the gutter; a match flared and, briefly, I saw a huddle of young boys crouched over silver paper. One looked up—and before the flame died, I saw his narrow, haunted face, as if he, too, was slowly changing into a rat. A policeman strolled past. He looked me up and down. I broke into a decisive walk, trying to appear as though I knew where I was going, but I didn't. I had no idea where to go or what to do. As soon as I was out of sight of the policeman, I stopped, hesitated, and glanced around fearfully. Perhaps I should go back and join the glue-sniffers, just to be with somebody. I felt as much an outcast as they were. I walked again, trying to appear purposeful, but I hesitated and stopped.

A man stepped out of the shadows. "Are you Monika?" he asked casually, lighting up a cigarette.

"No. Nina."

"Pity. Don't know what's happened to the girl. I was supposed to meet her. She's being employed to come and look after my grandmother." He walked slowly away. ". . . Must have missed the bus."

I knew I shouldn't but . . . "Excuse me!" I called out. I didn't want him to go. "Er—I, too, should have been met, but he's not here—and I know it's stupid—but I don't have his address—my cousin's . . ." I lied desperately. "I'm not sure what to do. Do you know a hostel or somewhere I can go? Just for the night? Then I can try and find him tomorrow."

He paused. I thought how the back of his head looked like my eldest brother Georgiu's, with those long black curls clustering at the nape of his neck. He turned around and stared directly at me. I could hardly breathe. In the weak, low lighting of the bus station, shadows enveloped him till he nearly disappeared. He ambled back as if he'd never meant to walk away. He had the languid confidence of a man who had been around and knew the ropes. It was not a handsome face—but somehow worldly; a face not young, but not yet old; the creases forming down the sides of his mouth, and across his brow, were faint and new. His blue eyes stood out against the strangely leathery brown skin—a skin you'd have expected to be that of a peasant farmer, rather than this somewhat sleekly dressed city slicker. I couldn't help noticing his hands; they, too, were muscular and roughened by hard work—laboring work. If he had hoped to pass for a city man, his hands gave him away. Just as a glimmer of doubt began to form in my mind, he smiled, and it was so full of warmth and reassurance I almost fell at his knees and kissed the hem of his coat. "Can you help me?"

"Well!" he said. "My girl didn't turn up. There's still a job available. Do you want to give it a try?"

"What makes you think I need a job?" I tried to sound strong and indignant.

"Don't you?"

"My cousin was going to help me—"

"What cousin?" he interrupted harshly. "I've heard it all."

"Sorry I bothered you. I can look after myself," I insisted, and turned on my heel, only to see the policeman returning.

I could hear myself emitting short panic-stricken squeals like a trapped animal. A hand gripped my elbow in a vise. It was the man of the shadows. He enfolded me like a lover, holding me close, and thrust me through the station doors, out into the sordid night. When it was safe again, he let me go; pushed me away, as one might push out a boat across a pond.

"Where do you want to spend the night? Here? In a doorway, under the arches, get moved on by the police—get raped?" He paused to let his words sink in; let the chill night get into my bones, and fear into my brain. "Or do you want to come with me? You'll get a bed—a roof over your head—and in exchange, you look after my grandmother. Her brain's going soft—you know. She forgets things; doesn't know the time of day; she wanders off. She needs constant supervision. See? I've found you the perfect solution. Of course you'll go when you find a better job—but jobs aren't so easy to come by. And you're rather young—you could easily fall into the wrong hands."

I felt like a time traveler; stranded on another planet; bewildered, afraid. I felt the tears trickling onto my cheeks.

He smiled. He knew he'd won. "Coming with me?"

I knew I shouldn't. I knew I shouldn't go with a stranger, but I didn't know what else to do. Who else could help me? But this was the start of my journey which would bring me to London.

Exhausted with her racing swim, Nettie rolled over onto her back, relaxing in the water, looking up at the reflections of water dancing in the gold of the ceiling. With growing sadness, she realized that even though she was always provided with playmates when needed—Marie-Claire in St. Tropez, Carmen in Ibiza, the Hauser twins in Hamburg, and Alice here in London—none of them were like the friends she read about in her books: friends who shared games and hobbies, friends who did everything together, friends who went to school together, and came home for tea, and sometimes stayed over. She realized she had no best friend, no one with whom she could share secrets. The only best friend she had ever really had was Miss Kovachev, who had seemed both child and adult all in one, and she had gone. Perhaps, she pondered, only if you went to school would you find a real best friend. Nettie flipped over into a breaststroke at the thought. Why shouldn't she go to school?

A slight shift of a palm caught her attention. She thought she glimpsed two golden eyes, watching her through the fronds. She stopped swimming and trod water, suddenly nervous. Was there someone? No! Only the reflection of sunlight glancing off the conservatory onto moist leaves, wasn't it? Her uneasiness still lingered when she emerged from the pool. She showered, dried and changed, and wandered back to the house, unwilling to rejoin the party.

She climbed the stairs and, reaching her floor, glanced over the banisters at the revelers. Out of the corner of her eye, she glimpsed a movement in the corridor below; as brief as a blink, parting the air with barely a ripple; yet she was sure it was him—the boy. He moved fast, and disappeared, not into Great-aunt's room this time, but farther along, into the television room.

She sped down the staircase to the second floor. The door to the television room was shut. She opened it slowly, silently. The long sweeping curtains were drawn, and the room was in semidarkness except for the glow of the huge television screen, set into the wall, turning the room into a home theatre.

A soccer match was taking place. The players seemed life-size as they hurtled across the screen, a red player tackling a blue. The huge bright screen cast a glow. She pushed the door farther open and peered inside. She couldn't see anyone. No one sat on the sofa, or in any of the comfy chairs scattered about. The room was empty.

He must be a ghost, thought Nettie nervously. She was about to close the door again but stopped dead. Sticking out from behind the curtain she glimpsed the tip of a shoe. Creeping silently across the thick, plush carpet, she reached the curtains and, with beating heart, yanked them apart.

"Ahhhh!" Nettie screamed and fell back.

"Ahhhh!" The ghost yelled, too.

Nettie scrambled for the door, but then looked back.

A boy with terrified eyes—a black boy—peered over the arm of the chair.

They stared at each other in shocked amazement. He got to his feet, clutching the curtains around him, as if wishing he could disappear, his expression veering from surprised to panic-stricken. He glanced around as if looking for a way to escape, then back to her. Finally Nettie asked weakly, "Are you a ghost?"

He emerged a little farther from behind the curtain, though still clutching it like a shield. She could see now that he was tall—much taller than she; he was slim and wiry, his tight, black curly-haired head rose smoothly from his neck, showing his pointy elflike ears. "I, er, I . . . No."

"Are you from the other side?" whispered Nettie.

"What?" He looked even more scared. He shook his head. "I'm from down below," he muttered.

"Down below? You mean from the underworld? From hell?"

"What you talking about? Me dad's Mr. Baldwin, yeh? You know, he's your doorman. We live down below in the basement; just me and him. Me mum went back to Barbados to look after Granddad. Gettit?"

Nettie frowned; the basement? She had never been in the basement—never even thought about it, as it was below sidewalk level; below the iron railings that looped along a narrow wall which dropped down about ten feet. She had never thought of Mr. Baldwin as being a person. He was just always there, sitting behind the desk in the reception hall, where he could monitor everyone who came and went. She never thought he might have another life; a wife in Barbados, and a son. She hadn't even known that Mr. Baldwin lived in the same building as she did; so much for her being a secret agent! The only secret she knew about Mr. Baldwin was that he kept a bag of toffees under the counter.

But, come to think of it, even Mr. Baldwin must have a bed he slept in, a room where he ate his dinner, a place, even, where he put his feet up and watched the television.

With a shock, Nettie realized she was not the only child in the house.

"Please don't tell," begged the boy. "Me dad would get the sack—and then we'd have to leave here. Gettit? I only came to see the telly. It's new, innit? I heard about it. Dad told me you've got this huge screen, yeh, and a satellite—so you can see fifty channels or more. And it's Manchester United against Chelsea, yeh. I really wanted to see the match, and our telly's only got four channels. Don't tell on me. Please. I'll get slaughtered."

With a sweeping gesture, he let go the curtain and stepped right out, his head tipped slightly to one side, smiling a charming smile, which showed his funny crooked teeth. "I love your swimming pool. Like Hollywood, innit? And your telly room; it's like having your own cinema, yeh!" He was trying to win her over.

"You're a spy. You've been watching me. You watched me swimming, didn't you!" cried Nettie accusingly.

"I did not," he protested, "not exactly." He grinned again; cheekily, impishly. "Hey, man, I know I'm not supposed to come up here, but . . ." He pulled a face.

"Have you come before?"

He shrugged. "Yeh . . . kind of . . . You're the one who visits that weird old ballet dancer, ain't yer?"

"So it was you! You're not a ghost. What a pity." Nettie was disappointed.

"Me, a ghost? I like that!" He looked up with a shout of laughter, his hands outspread. "Hit me if you like, yeh. You'll see I'm solid."

"Anyway, she's not weird. She's my aunt. She used to be famous and beautiful. Was it you, moving things around in her apartment? Was it you who moved my shoes? Was it you . . . ?" She paused. Her voice dropped. "Was it you tapping in the Round Tower and calling my name?"

"Well . . . sort of. Didn't hurt, did it?" He looked at her with wide, innocent eyes. "I never stole nothin', yeh."

"You mean, you *were* in the Round Tower? How dare you!" Nettie was outraged, yet there was a relief, too. It removed her fear of going back. "Oh, I see! It was you sneaking around our house, spying on us, maybe pinching things. If you were cheeky enough to go in the Round Tower—perhaps you've been in my bedroom, too. Shall I call my father?"

The smile vanished, as if he was alarmed that his charm hadn't worked. "I've never taken nothing. Moved things, yeh—but it was only a joke, man! Anyway—I wasn't *in* the Round Tower."

"I heard you. Don't lie."

"I'm not lying. I wasn't exactly *in* the Round Tower, yeh. I was outside."

"Oh—hanging from the window ledge?" jeered Nettie.

"I was at the back door."

"What back door? How can there be a back door four floors up?"

"Show you?" he said tentatively.

"Go on then," Nettie challenged.

The boy hesitated. "You'll tell on me."

"I won't."

"Promise or die?"

"Don't be stupid. I said I wouldn't. I promise, and I'm good at keeping promises and secrets."

"I dunno, man."

She stared at him defiantly. "You've got to show me, or . . ."

The boy relented. "You go first, then. Go to the Round Tower, yeh, and when I tap, go into the bathroom."

Nettie stared at him. Was he trying to make a fool of her? "All right, show me."

"I'll go my way. You go yours. I'll be there in a minute." And then he was gone, so fast that, by the time Nettie stepped out into the corridor, there was no sign of him.

Boy, not ghost. Her eyes were shining, like the crystals in the chandelier which hung over the guests below flitting across the marble floors, balancing glass and plate, chattering and laughing. Uncle Charlie was at the piano playing toe-tapping blues and boogie-woogie. "Hey, Charlie Boy, play us . . ." trilled a woman's voice. No one noticed Nettie as she ran upstairs to the Round Tower.

Once more, a strange silence pervaded the room. It was not the silence of stillness, but a silence which throbbed with the presence of someone who wasn't there. Nettie looked around her. How could the boy possibly get in? She sat down on Miss Kovachev's bed and waited, still a little afraid and disbelieving.

He was more than a minute. She checked her watch; three minutes, four minutes—he should be here soon, that's if he wasn't lying, and tricking her so that he could get away. But suddenly, there it was: *tap, tap, tap.* It came from the bathroom. "Nettie, Nettie!" came a breathy voice.

"Where are you? Stop scaring me!" hissed Nettie. "Come out."

Tap, tap, tap! It came from behind the cupboard door. "Nettie! Open the door." The cupboard contained a mop, a bucket, and bathroom cleansers. No sign of the boy. The tapping continued. It came from the back of the cupboard, and suddenly she realized she could see a handle. There must be another door! The handle lowered, and the door opened, tipping over the mop with a clatter.

"See? Didn't I tell you? Calling me a liar now, are you?" The boy's face peered around, grinning cheekily.

"How did you get in without being spotted by security, or your father, or Gimley?" Nettie was astonished and excited.

"I told yer. There are stairs, yeh? Back stairs; stone—not posh ones like the ones you use; and no cameras or bodyguards. I'll show yer. Come in here."

She stepped over the bucket and peered into the gloom beyond.

"There you are! The back stairs."

Nettie was astonished. "Why didn't I know?"

"The servants always used to use the back steps, but your dad put in another lift for us, yeh, so no one uses them now—'cept me."

I wonder if Miss Kovachev knew about them, pondered Nettie.

"Come on down. I'll take you to the second floor."

She followed him, one step at a time. They reached another door. It opened up behind a curtain guarded by an expansive, flowering potted plant. The sound of the party rushed through like a wave.

"Let's spy on them." On hands and knees, the boy crawled to the banister, flattening himself to the floor and peering down through the balustrade. "When I grow up, I'm going to be a secret agent."

"Me too," breathed Nettie, flopping down alongside him. "Or a ballet dancer, I haven't made up my mind. Do you have a code name? Mine's Point 007, not like James Bond—he's just 007. The point makes all the difference. It's one speck of stardust. Did you know we were made of stars? It's what Miss Kovachev said."

"Point 007?" scoffed the boy. "That's a good one." And they both broke into giggles, smothering them in their hands.

"I know every inch of this house," boasted the boy. "Bet I know it better than you. And I see things . . ."

"I see all sorts of things, too," whispered Nettie. "I saw you—I thought you were a ghost!" And they both choked with giggles again. "What's your name?"

"Benny. Benny the Phantom! Bet you've never slid down them banisters. I have."

"Go on then. Show me, I dare you!" hissed Nettie. "No one will notice."

"But if they do see me, that'll be an end to it, know what I mean? I'd never be able to come here again. I'll do it when there's no one around."

"I'm going to then." Nettie leaned over the banister on her stomach.

"Hey, wait!" Benny held her leg. "Look who's just arrived." He pulled her down and pressed his face up to the balustrade. "Paddy Potter. Pistol Paddy!" He spoke with awe.

"Pistol Paddy? Who's he?" whispered Nettie, noting the black-suited bodyguard towering above him in dark glasses.

"Oh, he's in the racket; a big fish, he is," breathed Benny knowledgeably.

Nettie didn't really know what the "racket" was. She sometimes heard her father say, "He's in the racket," or "He's legit," but his tone of voice didn't indicate if that was a good thing or a bad thing.

"He doesn't look very big," muttered Nettie, screwing up her nose.

"There's ways of being big, yeh!" whispered Benny.

Pistol Paddy was a small, pale, thin-faced man, with darting eyes and twitching hands. He looked overwhelmed by the beaver-skin coat draped over him, but when he tossed it off into Gimley's hands, his body seemed to leap out of his coat with the spring and strength of an acrobat, with gold and diamond rings flashing on his fingers. For a man so small, his voice was loud and booming as he strode up to Nettie's father. "Hey! Good to see you, Vlad. How's the business?"

"Good, good, Paddy." Vlad embraced him.

"He'll have a pistol inside his jacket pocket," whispered Benny. "Never without it. Your dad's taking him over to the judge—he's in the racket, so's that one there—chief of police, my foot, a bent copper he is—bent as a hairpin." Benny was enjoying showing off how much he knew.

Nettie saw Don sidling through the throng to greet Pistol Paddy with an overfamiliar slap on the back. "I know that one," proclaimed Nettie. "That's Don. I call him Don the Chimp. He's my tutor. Is he legit, or in the racket?"

"Don the Chimp?" There was almost a sneer in Benny's voice. "Don the Wimp, more like. Used to be legit, I think. He's in the racket now.

"That huge lump of flesh by the statue is Bernie the Hand; he runs casinos. And that's Father Gabriel."

"He's legit?" cried Nettie. It was like a guessing game.

"Nah! In the racket, of course! Even priests and bishops are in your father's racket."

"What does it mean?"

"Just that they work for your dad."

"But he's a priest!"

"What's that got to do with it?"

The party had got noisier with raucous laughter and rowdy voices. The drink flowed, cigar smoke rose up through the atrium, and Nettie watched her father with a different kind of fascination, mingling with his guests, slapping their backs, roaring with laughter; such a popular and genial host! Uncle Charlie had given way to a small jazz band which was playing full blast. "Uncle Charlie's in the racket, isn't he?" asked Nettie.

"Not him. He's legit," said Benny. "But that man he's talking to now is Eddie Schotts—Hot Shots—best bagman in town."

"Bagman for what?" asked Nettie. "Is he a porter?"

Benny grinned. "That's a good one! Hey! Do you know that one?" He pointed out a small, round podgy man with rimless spectacles who looked like a bank manager or a company director. "He's in the racket; comes to your house quite often. 'Dopey' they call him—but he ain't, yer know. Don't want to get on the wrong side of him. My dad says he's an enforcer."

"What's an—"

"Sugar! Someone's coming. I gotta get out of here." In a flash,

Benny had slithered away behind the curtain, and through the door to the back steps. Nettie pulled back the curtain. "Benny!" she hissed down the back stairs, though he had already vanished. "What's an enforcer?"

"Tell you later," came a mocking reply.

"Oh, miss!" Ella appeared at the far end of the corridor as Nettie backed away from the secret door. "Your mother's been looking for you everywhere!"

1

Down the Back of Beyond

Just as the world had seemed a different place out there in the park when she realized her mother had lied to her, so now the world seemed different yet again—here in this house. There was a basement home she hadn't realized existed and a ghost who was really a boy, living right here under her own roof. Phantom Benny! How silly it seemed now. Nanny was right about ghosts! And he knew things—secret things about the house; things about her father's friends: who was legit, and who was in the racket. She didn't know, didn't understand. Nothing was quite what it seemed anymore. Her mother had always been a certainty, but now? Nettie wanted to hold on to her in a way she hadn't since she was a young child, lies or no lies. Whenever she went away, Nettie felt a deep desolation. She loved her mother so much—yet how would she ever know when her mother was telling the truth? What was the difference between a white lie and a black lie?

And then there was Miss Kovachev's notebook hidden in the drawer beneath the bed. Had she forgotten it? Or had she meant Nettie to find it? But what was the use if Nettie couldn't read it? One thing which thrilled her was knowing there were back stairs; stairs which could take her out of the house into the world beyond—a world she longed to explore. Perhaps the stairs could lead her to Miss Kovachev.

One day, I'll find her and return the notebook, Nettie thought.

A few days later, Vlad was in Russia and Peachy had jetted off on a shopping spree to Milan. Nettie would have gone with her, but when Great-aunt grumbled, "You'll never be a real dancer if you flit off like that," she stayed behind. But how she wished her mother hadn't gone this time. Somehow, the fact that she had found her mother out in a lie meant she wanted to be with her even more. Nanny said people told white lies to protect others—so what was Mother trying to protect her from? Maybe Mother needed protecting, too. As she was leaving, Nettie had clung fiercely to her. "Don't go. You're my prisoner. I won't let you go ever, ever."

"Got to go, darling! I'll miss my flight." She gently untangled her daughter's arms from around her neck. "It's only for three days. But I asked Cook to make your favorite chocolate cake, and guess what?"

"What?" sighed Nettie, burying her face in her mother's pearl-strewn neck.

"Alice is coming to tea."

"I don't like Alice."

"Of course you do, sweetie. You're like sisters. You've known her since you were three."

"That doesn't mean I like her," muttered Nettie. "Why can't you shop in London?"

"Nettie Betty," her mother pretended to scold, "don't be like that. Here, give me a proper kiss. I'm taking Hepworth with me, so Tamas will be your bodyguard if you want to go to the park with Alice. Now be good, and don't forget to do your homework for

Don, and, sweetie, ask Nanny to get Andre to do something to your hair. You're beginning to look like the wild woman of Borneo," she cried as she whirled away.

Alice came and went. They had swum in the pool, watched television, and eaten Cook's chocolate cake. Alice was all right, but was always going on about her latest designer T-shirt, or shoes, or party dress, or ski outfit. She was beginning to wear makeup and wanted to show Nettie her new eyeliner and, what's more, "I've got a boyfriend. Guess who? Jack Courtney!" she exclaimed without waiting for Nettie to guess.

She had prattled on and on, hardly noticing that Nettie was silent, full of feelings of uncertainty and unanswered questions.

After Alice left, Nanny retired to her room to watch her favorite television program, while Nettie struggled with homework for Don. At last it was done, and she went along to the schoolroom to leave it for him on his desk.

The schoolroom was slowly being enveloped in darkness when she arrived. She didn't bother to turn on the light as she had only intended to drop her work on his desk and then leave, but a single star blazed through the window at the back of the room, which overlooked the park. She walked over to get a clearer view. Jupiter was it? It looked so huge—like a giant galactic flower surrounded by a glow, its light streaming down on the park. "I am made of starlight," she breathed softly.

How often Miss Kovachev and she had stood beneath a night sky, gazing up at the different galaxies and stars. Miss Kovachev seemed to know them all. "There's Venus, Eve's bright star! There's Mars, named after the God of War—see, it does have a warlike glow, the color of blood! And look, far up there, you can see the twins, Castor and Pollux!" She had pointed out the constellations: the Plow, the

Bear, and glittering Orion with his belt. "I wish you could see the Milky Way—but the city is so bright, the sky is so polluted, that now we see so few stars. You should come to my country. I could take you up into the mountains, to a peak where there is no artificial light; where there is real darkness, real night, and you would see the Milky Way with the naked eye; swooping across the heavens, a dazzling path made up of millions of stars!"

Nettie remembered those words with a shock. It was perhaps the only time Miss Kovachev had talked about where she came from: *my country*. But where was her country? Oh why had she never asked? What a stupid ignorant girl she was; how selfish never to have asked anything about Miss Kovachev; if she had any family, or where she came from. Was she legit? Or was she in the racket?

Tears began to fall as Nettie felt so much was out of her control. She had lost Miss Kovachev, and she couldn't even hold on to her mother when she most needed her.

There was a sound of footsteps approaching. Instinctively, she stepped behind the curtain, unwilling for anyone to find her in tears.

The footsteps entered; they were heavy, like a man's. He didn't put on the main light, but walked to the desk and switched on a lamp. Nettie peered around the curtain. It was Don. She saw him pick up her homework, then, with a sigh, toss it to one side as though it didn't matter. He opened his desk and brought out his laptop. The glow of the screen cast a blue light around the room. He sat down and began to type. He typed fast, stooping over the keyboard.

After a while he paused, leaned back, and removed his spectacles; he enfolded his head in his arms. His fingers crept over his skull, rotated over his bald patch, moved down around his neck, rubbing and caressing. His arms entwined and crossed as if he was embracing himself, and now, in the shadowy light, they looked like serpents coiling around him. He massaged his arms, sliding down to his wrists and fingers. He no longer looked like Don the Chimp or Don the Wimp, but as if, at any moment, he would turn into a writhing snake.

Nettie shuddered. Abruptly he ceased, replaced his spectacles, and began typing again. Nettie felt her legs beginning to cramp. She had stayed too long, and seen too much; but she couldn't just step out and let him know she was there. She stared up at the stars. *I am starlight, I am starlight,* she said to herself over and over.

When the cell phone went off she almost cried out; its jingle shattered the silence, freezing the heartbeat. She recognized the call ring; it was a tune from *Swan Lake*—her favorite melody. She hated him for having her favorite music as his ring tone. It played louder and louder, demanding attention. He fumbled in his jacket pocket and yanked it out. The tune ceased mid-phrase as he flipped open the lid. "Barney? Yes. She's been seen. Yes . . . In the park . . . What the devil? . . . The child saw her."

Me? Does he mean me?

"What's going on? You've lost her? Oh my God!" Don cursed. "He's spitting blood. Well you'd better sort it out pronto. Sort it, do you hear?" There was a pause; he listened; a kind of hiss escaped from his lips; the pause lengthened; he shrank into himself, and his free hand began fretfully to massage the top of his head, finger down his neck and around his face. "You'd better find her or, heaven knows, someone's going to get impaled for this, most likely me. But whatever happens to me will happen to you. Believe me." He snapped shut the phone. For a moment he sat curled into himself like a stone gargoyle, the light and shadows chiseling out a face of fury and fear. As if finding his spine, he suddenly straightened, closed the laptop with a click, extinguished the light, and was gone. Nettie waited till she was certain he wouldn't come back, then crept forward, checked the corridor, and fled to the Round Tower. Miss Kovachev's room was bathed in moonlight, so she didn't switch on the light till she got to the bathroom. She opened the bathroom cupboard. Did she dare? There was only one person she wanted to see, and that was Benny. But that meant going down the back stairs to the basement.

"Come on, Point 007," she said to herself, as she stepped nervously over the bucket and mop to reach the door which opened to the stone steps. The bathroom light lit up the first few steps, but they curved away into pitch darkness. She should have picked up a flashlight. James Bond would never have been so careless. But she couldn't go back and risk running into anyone. Slowly, slowly, with her back pressed against the wall, feeling for each step first with her foot, she began to descend.

Mr. Baldwin's voice halted her with a shock; a shaft of light lit up the darkness as, below her, a door opened.

"Right, son! See you later."

She heard a door close, and the light was extinguished; relief. Plunged back into darkness, Nettie edged around the curve of the wall, down a few more steps, and suddenly it was level. No more steps. She had reached the bottom. A light gleamed through the crack of a door ahead. Tentatively she knocked, without preparing any excuse if it turned out to be the wrong door. Too late! 007 would never have made that mistake either. An eye peered at her through the spyhole in the door; the handle turned and the door opened an inch on the chain. "Nettie! It's you! Man! I thought it was a rat. Nobody ever knocks on this door." He unhooked the chain and let her in. "What are you doing here?"

"A rat?" Nettie squealed. "You don't have rats, do you?"

"Well, not the squeaky, nippy kind of rats, but vermin. You know! It's what your dad calls his enemies, like Borkoff and Pinelli—they're rats."

"What kind of enemies?" Nettie was alarmed. "I didn't know Daddy had enemies."

"Come in! Lucky for you, Dad's doing night duty tonight." Benny yanked her inside, closed the door, and replaced the chain. Nettie edged her way into a narrow hallway. It was a bit dingy, with a dusty mirror and a row of hooks for coats, but she hardly took anything in as she gabbled on about what she had overheard.

"Benny, I was in the schoolroom, and Don came in. I didn't want him to see me, so I hid. He phoned someone. I think he was talking about me seeing Miss Kovachev. He was angry and scared, and, Benny, he made *me* so scared. It's funny to hear only half a conversation, but it seemed like they had lost someone—lost *her*. They must have meant Miss Kovachev, and if they lost her, it means she was with them—people Don knows—and he said they had to find her. Do you think she ran away from them? That's how it sounded."

Benny shrugged with a frown, but said nothing.

"He said *the child saw her*. That must be me. If Miss Kovachev ran away, then she must be in danger." Nettie paused. Her face was white in the gloomy light. "They must have meant me, don't you think?"

"Dunno," muttered Benny. "Could be. Maybe. Maybe not." He didn't seem very interested.

She bit the inside of her lip, hardly wanting to ask. "What did you mean when you said my dad has enemies? What enemies?" she said finally.

Benny stared at her for a moment, as if unsure what to say. "Just enemies; people, you know what I mean? Who don't like him; in business, you know. But no worries! No one messes with your dad, yeh—not Vlad the Impaler."

"Vlad the Impaler?" Nettie repeated. *Impaled* was the word Don had used. Funny how you hear a new word, and then it seems everyone is using it. "Don said if they didn't find her he'd be impaled. What did he mean?"

"There was this guy, yeh, from Transylvania; a count called Vlad who lived in a castle up in the mountains. He had a thing about sitting down to dinner surrounded by people he had impaled on spikes. He liked to have them hanging from the walls while he ate. He liked their screams and moans, and blood dripping from their bodies." Benny relished the words, licking his lips all around with his tongue, and wriggling his fingers menacingly. "It increased his appetite. People say he was Count Dracula, the vampire, who sucked the blood of beautiful girls and turned them into vampires, too. Funny, innit?" Benny pulled back his lips and bared his teeth, sucking his breath in and out.

"That's not funny," protested Nettie furiously. "It's a horrible thing to say about my father, even as a joke. Especially as he's the kindest person I know."

"Not that you know many people, yeh?" quipped Benny.

Nettie looked affronted.

"Only joking, man! Yeh! Sorry. You did ask! I was only trying to tell you if anyone messes with your dad, yeh? Puts a foot wrong, you know what I mean? He nails them! So his enemies are scared of him. Gettit?"

"Dad can't have any real enemies. How silly." She laughed, but added, "Does he?"

"Everyone has enemies—even friends have enemies. Your dad

has—well let's put it like this, yeh—*business* enemies. Man, don't you realize how big your dad is? The bigger you are, the more enemies you have—that's what my dad said."

"Does your dad know everything?"

"Yeh, man! Almost everything."

"Did he know Miss Kovachev?" Nettie asked quietly.

" 'Spect so."

"Does he know why she left? Did he tell you?"

"Nope. He's not supposed to gossip, yeh. But look, stop worrying. Don works for your father, yeh! So he's not your enemy. Forget what you heard. You probably got it all backwards anyway. You shouldn't have come here. My dad would kill me if he knew you was here."

"You've crept around my house, so why shouldn't I creep around yours?" She tried to sound defiant, but her eyes were filled with tears and her brow streaked with anxiety.

"Well then, let me show you around, m'lady!" he exclaimed with a theatrical bow. "This is where we live. Not big, is it? We could all fit just into your bedroom!"

Benny opened one door: "The lounge, m'lady!" His arm swept around a small living room which opened to a dining-breakfast area, with French doors to a small paved garden and backyard. A sofa faced an artificial log-burning fire, flanked on either side by two armchairs. Standing free in one corner was a smallish television—now she could see why Benny loved the family one upstairs. But this was such a dear little home; so cheery with table lamps gleaming in the corners, a smell of food, a supper just eaten, the television showing a film, and Benny smiling. Here all her fears seemed like phantoms; just nightmares.

He led her back through the narrow hallway to another door opposite. The door couldn't open fully, as a double bed filled almost the entire room. A curtain hung across one side, shielding a hanging space and drawers. "Mum and Dad's room!" announced Benny. He took her out again and to what looked like a cupboard under the stairs. "De dummmm! My bedchamber!"

Nettie beamed with astonishment. "How sweet! It's so tiny—like a doll's house."

"Yeh—well it would look like a doll's house to you with your mansions and castles." Benny scowled.

"But I love it!" cried Nettie. "I like small rooms. That's why I wanted the Round Tower. Yours is like a cabin for one of the bodyguards on our yacht."

"Yeh! Well"—he sounded placated—"me dad built it. Look, he built me a study underneath with a place for my computer and schoolbooks, and basket drawers here for my clothes."

"Who's that?" Nettie pointed at a poster surrounded by team badges and a soccer scarf.

"Can't believe you don't know him! Rio Ferdinand of course! He plays for Manchester United. Signed, too," he boasted.

She peered at an open exercise book, full of names and numbers.

"Nosy!" he cried, slamming it shut.

"Why can't I see?"

"None of your business, that's why."

"Who's your teacher? Is it Don?"

"Don? No, man! You must be joking. I go to school."

"School? Do you go to school?"

"Of course. 'Ave to. Every kid does. Well, most."

"I don't," said Nettie.

"Yeh—well you're different, know what I mean? There's not many like you. Even royal kids go to school."

"Do you like it?"

"Mostly. I'm always having a laugh with me mates, yeh? I'd rather be at school than be taught at home with Don, I'll tell you that for nothing."

"I don't like Don," said Nettie. She studied Benny's face; she hardly knew him—yet felt he was her friend.

"He's not Miss Kovachev, that's for sure."

"No." She sighed. "I'm sure Don was talking about Miss Kovachev—and telling someone I had seen her in the park."

"Did you?" asked Benny.

"It looked like her. Mama said it wasn't but"—and she continued in a small voice, as if ashamed of what she was saying—"I think she was telling me a lie."

"Adults are always lying. Why don't you ask your dad?"

"I sort of did—when it happened, he didn't want to talk about it."

"Yeh—I suppose there was quite a bit of aggravation when Miss Kovachev left. Upset me dad. He nearly lost his job."

"Why?" asked Nettie. "Tell me!"

"Your dad thought my dad should have known about it; seen her, been able to stop her. He's security, yeh? But look, I don't know nothing. Just that she left without asking. No one does that in this house, know what I mean? She was here one minute, then gone. Scarpered. Never told no one. You just don't do that to your dad. She must have used these back stairs, yeh? Otherwise, the cameras would have picked her up. But that's all I know, I don't know why she left, how she left, or where she went. Anyway—it was ages ago. Don was probably talking about something completely different. I told yer—he's in the racket."

"I don't really know what the racket is. What does it mean, Benny? Don sounded so angry, it was frightening."

"Business, Nettie. Business. Like I said, it's what your dad's in. That's what they call it."

"Is your father in the business?"

"My dad?" Benny looked thoughtful. "Not really. He's worked for Vlad for years. He's just the doorman. We were in your last London house, you know—don't suppose you even saw us. But maybe I'll be in the business when I leave school. They always need secret agents."

"You mean, in the racket?"

"Sort of." Benny looked vague, as if he wasn't sure himself about the racket. "Dad wants me to be legit. Do well at school, go to university. Me? University? That's a laugh. I expect you'll go into your dad's business, yeh."

"I think I'm going to be a ballerina," said Nettie, "though I might be a spy. If I was a spy, we could both be in the business. But where's your school?"

"Across the park."

"Do you go on your own?"

"Course!" said Benny nonchalantly.

"Lucky thing. Wish I could go out on my own. Don't you even have a bodyguard?"

"Bodyguard? Are you joking? I'm not rich like you. No one would want to kidnap me."

Kidnap. The word had a shuddery, frightening ring to it. Why would anyone ever want to kidnap her? She thought of Miss Kovachev. "Maybe she was kidnapped!" she exclaimed out loud.

"Who?"

"Miss Kovachev. Maybe that's why she ran away from them."

The grin on Benny's face faded. "You don't half go on about her," he muttered. "Girls come and go here, yeh. You know that."

"Maids and au pairs come and go, but not Miss Kovachev—she was different. She wasn't one of those. She stayed."

Benny looked uneasy. "She's probably gone home to Bulgaria, just like your mum said."

"Bulgaria? Mama said she'd gone to Bulgaria, not gone home!" Nettie frowned.

"But that's where she came from, innit? Oh, forget it."

Bulgaria! A thought struck her. *Was the notebook written in Bulgarian?*

"Benny! What does Bulgarian look like? Have you ever seen it?" cried Nettie excitedly.

"Nah! Could Google it, I suppose. What d'you wanna see that for?"

"Oh, Benny, please. Please find some. I just want to see it!"

Benny sat down in front of his computer, went to his browser, and typed in *Bulgaria*. His fingers flew over the keyboard and then he clicked through the search results with his mouse. A Bulgarian Web site came up.

Съе Република България

дине

нието прави силата

"Gobbledygook," muttered Benny. "It's all backwards."

"It looks the same," breathed Nettie.

"Same as what?"

"Oh—just a book I saw her reading," mumbled Nettie. Somehow

she wasn't ready to tell him about the notebook. It felt like giving away Miss Kovachev's secret.

Benny looked thoughtful. "Maybe she was in the racket, yeh?"

"Of course she was, silly. She was my tutor. You said being in the racket meant working for Dad—well?"

This was getting too deep. Benny pushed back his chair violently. Enough was enough.

"Benny! What's up?" Nettie was bewildered.

"I'm not even supposed to talk to you, you know. Your dad would chuck us out if he found out you'd been here—and asking questions all the time. You're too nosy." He got up and strode out. "Wanna drink?"

"Sorry!" she sang, trailing after him to the kitchen. "I won't tell anyone, you know. But you don't really think Miss Kovachev was in the racket, do you?"

"Oh I dunno, Nettie. Forget it, won't you? Have a Coke." He yanked open the fridge. "Look, when you've had that, I've got to get my homework done."

"Wish I could go to school with you," sighed Nettie, opening her soda. "Does Peckham drive you?"

"I take the tube and walk a bit."

The tube. The underground; Nettie thought about trains rushing beneath her feet. She wondered if they would be cutting through those underground meadows that Miss Kovachev used to tell her about. And how did it cross those underground rivers? The thought of it sounded frightening.

"I've never been on the underground." Nettie found her mind fleeing the house, her home, which suddenly felt, as it had never felt before, strangely oppressive; a house of secrets—and she had thought all the secrets were hers.

"What! You ain't never been on the underground?" Benny was incredulous. "How old did you say you were?" He thrust a biscuit into her hand.

"Thirteen. Nearly," replied Nettie defensively. "Why should I have been on the underground? It's smelly, dirty, and crowded. Only riffraff go on the underground—that's what Mama says."

" 'That's what Mama says,' " mimicked Benny cruelly. "Am I riffraff, then?"

"Course not!" Nettie was mortified.

"Then don't go saying things which you don't know nothing about. Don't suppose your mama has ever been on the underground either, so how should she know?"

"I've never been to the Antarctic, but I know it's full of ice and snow," Nettie declared.

"Hey! How about I take you on the underground? Then you can see for yourself. Your dad's away, yeh? Your mum? She's gone to Milan, yeh? We can sneak out. No one will ever know." His eyes glittered with the thought. "I know how to get you in and out without no one seeing you."

"What about Swivel-Eyes? I never go anywhere without him. He's my bodyguard when Mama's away. He'll never let me," murmured Nettie.

"Oh, forget him. He's off duty at ten o'clock. You're in bed by nine-thirty, don't forget."

"The cameras will see us."

"I know how to get around them, no probs!" Benny stated boastfully.

"I'm not sure . . ." Nettie faltered at the thought. She had always been an amenable and obedient girl. This idea was bad. Very bad, and she knew, if anyone found out—Nanny, her parents, or Tamas—

they'd be furious. And besides—think of the danger. "What if I did get kidnapped?" she cried.

"I told you! I'll be your bodyguard. Trust me."

"Don't know why anyone would want to kidnap me anyway," sniffed Nettie.

"Money, of course."

"When do you want to go?"

"Tonight."

"Oh, I couldn't."

"Why not? My dad is working nights, so he won't know I've gone. Does anyone check on you after you've gone to bed?"

"Nanny does, after half an hour, because I always read a bit. She turns off my light. That's it."

"She never comes back?"

"Only if I call her or if I'm ill."

"Well then, we leave after your nan's turned out the light. We'll go for a whirl on the underground, and be back before midnight—just like Cinderella!"

Nettie gulped down her Coke. "I'll think about it."

"Tonight's the best, what with both your mum and dad away," advised Benny. "Now scram, will yer! I've got to get going." He opened the door into the hallway, suddenly keen for her to go. "Must get on with my homework. You have a cell phone, don't yer? Text me later when you've made up your mind," he said, giving her his number before almost pushing her out.

After she'd gone, Benny rushed back to his computer. What he hadn't told Nettie was that he had been hacking into the house computers for a long time, just for fun; it was what secret agents did. He'd learned a lot from Tommy Tinker, one of Vlad's security men—before he vanished, that is—a bit like Miss K. One day he was there—the next gone. "Probably tied to concrete at the bottom of some river," joked Swivel-Eyes. Trouble was, Tinker was a boaster—even to a kid like Benny. Liked to show off. "I could get into the Pentagon, if I wanted!" he had bragged, and he showed Benny quite a few tricks. Now Nettie had given him a reason to go hacking; see if he could find out what happened to Miss Kovachev. Pity Tinker wasn't around. He'd find out in seconds. Like, for instance, how had Vlad found Miss Kovachev?

Everyone knew that Vlad was mainly in real estate: hotels, casinos, apartments; that he had a transport business right across Europe, and an employment agency. He had his fingers in many pies. Benny looked at the lists of numbers and words he had been compiling for a long time now—just as Tommy had shown him—combinations that could make up passwords. It made him feel good; made him feel powerful, knowing things about everyone. But best of all, Tommy had told him all about installing back doors to hack right in. "Start with your dad's computer," he had advised. "You can load a back-door program and get remote control, and then it's yours! You can go into everything: files, spreadsheets, accounts—everything. Well—almost everything. You'll come up against antivirus stuff all the time—and they change, but that's the fun of it!"

Benny got into his father's—that was easy—then he got into Tamas's and Peckham's. That's how he got to know that another of Vlad's interests was an au pair agency, and that many of the girls stayed at a halfway house run by Father Gabriel. Father Gabriel arranged work permits, visas, and passports through his M.P. friend, who knew people in the immigration services and who would, for a fee, make the right contacts and arrange for passports and visas. Sometimes, in brief, one-line e-mails, Benny would learn that Pistol Paddy was sent to sort something out, or Hot Shots Eddie was put on standby.

What started out as a game became an obsession. His aim had always been to break into Vlad's computer. Even Tommy Tinker said that would be a triumph, but so far, he hadn't managed it. How did Vlad make his millions? That's what he wanted to know. Perhaps he could learn something. Perhaps one day, his dad wouldn't have to go on being a doorman forever, and Benny vowed it's what he would never be when he grew up. But for the moment, he must focus. Focus on any mention of Miss Kovachev. Focus on Don.

Don had a lot of anti-hacker software. Benny's fingers flew over the keys, jotting down words on the pad next to him. He knew it was only a matter of being patient until he cracked the codes.

8

THE UNDERGROUND

After fumbling her way back up the stone stairs, Nettie sat for a while on the round bed to think about Benny's proposal. It seemed mad. The thought of sneaking out of the house at night to go on the underground was like an impossible fantasy. Nettie struggled with the dilemma. Never before had she been faced so directly with doing something she knew her parents wouldn't allow. She wanted to; she shouldn't; but what if she saw Miss Kovachev? The thought of the back stairs—the secret stairs leading out into the wide, wide world—was enticing. *Come on, Point 007,* a voice spoke inside her head. *You won't find her by staying at home. Get out there.*

With a big sigh of a decision being made, she sent Benny a text. I'LL GO.

OK. TXT ME LTR WEN REDY. WIL FTCH U, he replied.

Back in her room, Nettie slipped out onto her balcony, just as she used to with Miss Kovachev, and looked up at the moon. It was strangely low, so low that it even seemed to be descending, coming down, down, down; as if about to engulf the earth in an almighty collision.

Nettie was almost choking with apprehension. She could always change her mind, she thought comfortingly. After Ella had run the bath, Nanny came to see Nettie to bed. She looked so safe and normal. "Can you read Bulgarian, Nanny?"

"Course not! What a question. English is quite enough for me, thank you very much. Whatever made you ask that?"

"Just wondered."

She just wondered. She wondered now about the times, when she was younger, she had overheard Peachy and Vlad speaking in another language. They had laughed and said that there were occasions when grownups wanted to say things they didn't want nosy little girls to understand; that it was their own private language, and gave it no name.

She got into bed, hiding her cell phone under her pillow. She hoped that Nanny didn't see her nervous agitation. She opened her book as she always did, and Nanny kissed her good night before going to her own rooms. In about half an hour, Nanny would come and check that her bedside light was off, and that would be it.

She read Harry Potter. It was about magic and magicians, but it was also about going to school. She lay back on her pillow and dozed. She had a fitful dream about going to a school; a school where everyone spoke a different language, and she couldn't understand them. She awoke with a start. The light was off. Nanny had been in. Her cell phone had beeped under her ear with a message. She switched the light on again. The book which had been clutched in her hands had been gently removed and set on the table beside her.

WHAT'S UP? said the message.

Checking her watch, she saw with dismay that it was already half past ten. She hoped it wasn't too late.

SORRY. FELL ASLEEP. NANNY GONE. READY, she texted back.

ON WAY MLADY, came the cheeky reply.

She flung herself out of bed and changed swiftly into jeans and a sweater, and turned off the light. It was a mild autumn night, and no rain, but still she took a rainproof jacket out of the wardrobe, and waited.

Her bedroom door opened silently. A flashlight beamed around the room. Benny was a hooded outline wearing jeans and sneakers. There was a whispered "Ready?"

She looked scared.

"You can always say no if you've changed your mind," Benny muttered. "Don't worry. I know what to do. We won't get caught."

"Is it too late to go?"

"Plenty of time! But hurry up," he urged her. "Not a word till we're out. We'll go from the Round Tower."

She sidled past him into the corridor.

The huge moon thrust its light through the slitted windows of the Round Tower as they quickly crossed from the bedroom into the bathroom. Benny opened the door to the back steps, and down they went to the basement.

Benny led her through his flat to the back. "This way!" He pointed to a door in the wall across the yard. "Through there— and—that's it! But see that camera up on the roof? Watch it while it pans across. It mustn't catch you. I'll dodge it and have the door open. We wait for it to pass. When I give you the signal, run. Gottit?"

She nodded nervously. "Gottit."

Nettie watched him become an opaque shadow as he crossed the yard. He glanced up casually at the camera on the roof, paused, then signaled.

"Now!"

She dashed across the kitchen yard and out into the street. He took her arm and propelled her swiftly away from the house and around the corner.

"See! It was easy."

Benny strode down the road, with Nettie half jogging behind him. They turned left, and left again, and everything changed from a silent, leafy, moonstruck back road to a main street, flooded with lights and shops and restaurants, and buses, taxis, cars, and pedestrians that flowed like a glittering river. "We'll go to Regent's Park station, then we're off."

Nettie had been along this road many times, but mostly by car—and never without a grownup. She felt an unexpected twinge of terror. Swivel-Eyes wasn't somewhere behind her as usual. She shrank close to Benny, wondering if this passerby or that knew who she was and might suddenly snatch her away.

They reached the ticket office in the tube station. "You'll need three quid, yeh," said Benny, fumbling in his pocket.

"Money?" Nettie was aghast. "You never said I needed money! I don't have any."

"You what? I thought your pockets would be stuffed with fifty-pound notes—oh man!" Benny groaned, shaking his head with astonishment. "Come to think of it, they say the Queen never has any money on her. I should have known."

"What do we do now?" asked Nettie, mortified. "Can't we go?"

"Well, as it so happens—" Benny grinned his grin, with which she was becoming so familiar, and with a flourish he pulled out a ten-pound note. "Means we can't go to the opera, m'lady! But we can do the tube."

Benny bought the tickets, showed her how to slot hers through the machine. The gates swung open, and they were in. He dragged her over to a tube map. "Seeing as how it's your first time, I think we should take this brown line, change on to the snazzy silver line, then on to that blue line, the red line, the black line, to the yellow line, and on to the brown line again, and der-dum back to where we started! You'll have had a go on almost all the lines! Good planning, eh?" Benny looked as proud as a peacock.

Nettie felt like a swimmer caught in a current from which she couldn't break free. Never had she been immersed in so many people, sweeping her along: up and down steps, along tiled tunnels; past wild buskers playing throbbing guitars or echoing saxophones, whose tumultuous rhythms chased after them as they stepped on and off escalators, and leaped between the sliding doors of the tube trains. Nettie sat silent with wonder. The train rushed through the black tunnels. Faces were reflected in the dark glass, and people spied on each other secretly. Their car hurtled into the bright lights of a station, jerking to a standstill; through doors opening, and doors closing, humanity flooded in and out—people of all sorts, such as she had never seen before; people her mother called riffraff!

Riffraff or not, they were full of evening cheerfulness. There were a few children with adults, though not many, and Nettie felt eyes sweeping over her and Benny, as if people were wondering what two children were doing out alone so late at night. But it was like a special ride at the fair, like a roller coaster or a ghost train, and she soon lost her terror of the escalators; they joined the people gliding upwards and downwards, like angels on Jacob's ladder.

And so it was, as she and Benny stood on an upward escalator, that Nettie spotted a woman in a purple head scarf on a down escalator. Her heart lurched. As they passed each other, the woman turned her head away.

"Miss Kovachev! Benny, it's her! Miss Kovachev!" She gripped his arm.

"Oh, not again!" Benny groaned.

"Miss Kovachev!" she yelled. "It's me, Nettie! Please! Please turn around." If the woman heard, she never turned around, and the escalator carried her inexorably to the bottom. Nettie tried running down the up escalator.

"Hey, watch it!" grumbled a man. "You'll cause an accident like that, young woman."

"Nettie, stop! You can't do that. We'll have to carry on to the top, and go back down," Benny howled with annoyance.

Nettie ran frantically up the up escalator, followed by Benny. By the time she got to the top, she was gasping and clutching herself with a stitch in her side. Benny pulled her around onto the opposite escalator, and they clattered down as fast as they could. They reached the bottom, but didn't know which way to go. They pushed their way through the crowd to one platform. Nettie scanned the people. A train came in. People surged towards the opening doors. She couldn't see the woman, and when the train went out again, the platform was empty. They checked the other platform. The train hadn't yet come in. Then she glimpsed the purple head scarf bobbing among the crowds. There was the roar of an incoming train.

"Miss Kovachev!" Nettie thrust her way towards her, in and out of the expectant passengers. "It's me, Nettie!" The train hurtled in. "Miss Kovachev!" she screamed.

The doors opened. The people surged forward. Nettie reached out to grab her arm. The woman bowed her head and jostled forward into the carriage. Nettie tried to follow, when a hand gripped her elbow and she felt herself dragged backwards. More passengers thrust themselves in front of her, squeezing themselves through the doors closing between them. The train pulled away as Benny came panting up.

"Hey, man! I thought I'd lost you. What do you think you're doing?" He dragged her away from the edge of the platform. "Never bringing you again. You're either getting mangled on the escalators or mashed up under a train."

"Why did you stop me? We could have got on the train with her," raged Nettie.

"What do you mean? I never stopped you! You'd got ahead of me, man! You gave me a flipping heart attack taking off like that."

"It was her—I know it was."

"Yeh, yeh!" scoffed Benny. "Didn't look like her to me. And oh man! If it had been her, she'd have turned around what with you yelling and shouting her name like that. Come on. We've got to get away before we get hauled off by the police or something."

"But . . . I'm sure it was her. I nearly touched her; someone pulled me back—"

"Everyone pushes and shoves on the underground. You're seeing her because you want to see her." There was almost a sneer in Benny's voice. "She's gone. Forget it."

"I know she's in London. I just know." Nettie stared over her shoulder into the black empty tunnel.

Benny grabbed her elbow. "Come on, man! We've got to get home, yeh?"

Home. How safe that word sounded. Home was when they had crept back inside Benny's basement flat, avoiding the camera's searching eye. Home was the back stone steps which led upwards, with Benny leading her by flashlight. Home was even the cupboard in the Round Tower, out of which they crept like house mice. Home was the landing on the third floor.

They crept around the atrium. The hollowed-out space in the heart of the house was in darkness, except for the crystals in the great chandelier, which caught the light from the dimmed lamps in the corridors and reflected in mirrors, glimmering like pale stars until they reached Nettie's door.

"See yer later," whispered Benny, and Nettie let herself into her room and shut the door. She stood in the darkness. Home. But where was Miss Kovachev? Where was *her* home at this moment? Without putting on the light, Nettie mechanically got undressed and rolled into bed.

Benny paused in the corridor. Had Nettie really seen Miss Kovachev? And had someone pulled Nettie back? He was keen to get to his computer and go on hacking, but a sound from far down below made him drop to his knees; a slight creak, a sigh, drew him to the banister. He peered into the gloom. His father sat on duty at his table, in a soft pool of light, glancing from time to time at a set of screens which received the pictures from all the security cameras around the house. A murmur of sounds, voices, soft, yet rising, reached his ears. He drew back as his father raised his head and got to his feet, his body straining and alert. Vlad's study door opened. A bright yellow light flashed across the marble floor, like the tail of a comet piercing the darkness. A figure stepped into the shaft of light, an overcoat was draped over his shoulders . . .

Vlad? Can't be. He's in Russia. Benny stared hard. *Is it him?*

Then the front door opened. There was an overlapping of shadows as other figures appeared, jostling inside. *Don! What's Don doing there?* And another man he didn't know. They held a woman between them. Benny nearly gasped out loud. Wasn't that the woman from the tube? Her head was down, her hair fell out from beneath a purple head scarf, covering her face, and she looked as if she was being half carried.

"Get her out of here! Should never have brought her to this house . . . idiot!"

"But, Boss, I thought you wanted to question her."

"Yes, but not here, you fool. Send her to Father Gabriel with the others. Use the back stairs."

"I'll see to it, Boss. Sorry, Boss." The unknown man's voice was whiningly apologetic. He tried to prop up the sagging woman. Don went to the other side of her and, between them, they dragged her to a door at the rear of the hall. In seconds, they were gone.

The figure stood motionless, casting a vast sinister shadow across the floor. He raised his arms. The shadow expanded up the walls like a giant bat spreading its wings. It seemed to levitate; rising through the glimmering atrium, through time and space; coming for him.

Blood whined in his ears. Benny shrank into a crouch; kneeling, supplicating, feeling a most appalling terror. His head dropped onto his arms in hopeless surrender. When he raised his head at last, the figure had gone, the shaft of light was extinguished.

Below, he watched his father take out a handkerchief and wipe his brow. Slowly, almost like an old man, he returned to his place behind the desk to continue his night duty. Sitting in the small circle of light which fell from his table lamp, he looked unutterably lonely. He scribbled something on a piece of paper, picked up the telephone, and tapped out a number. "Vlad's just sent them on their way. Be there in half an hour." He reached for his bag of toffees on a shelf under the desk and, with fumbling fingers, unwrapped one and put it in his mouth, like one who might have preferred to light up a cigarette.

Vlad. That's what his father had said. *So he was home.* Benny shuddered again.

9

Nightmares

Coiled into her bed, Nettie seethed with fears, questions, and uncertainty. Her restless sleep was tumbling with mixed-up dreams of rushing escalators turning into waterfalls, tipping her into rivers that swept her away. A flock of snow white swans beat their wings somewhere above her head. Running along the bank, a figure in a head scarf called out to her with alarm. "Nettie, Nettie!"

Another figure pursued her—something dark, batlike with vast outstretched wings, which swooped upon her and enveloped her in its embrace, and with a swoosh, a shining black swan rose into the air.

Nettie tried to cry out. "Miss Kovachev!"

He held my elbow, and with a nod to the policeman, who reappeared, eyeing us suspiciously, I allowed him to propel me into the night. We walked for an hour down empty streets, empty except for a few drunks reeling about, bundles of bodies that stirred in alcoves, and shadowy girls who first stepped out and then sank back into the blackness of doorways. He asked my name, and I asked his. "Kusa," he replied. He took me to a small apartment in a shabby, ill-lit district, where vagrant children scurried down dark lanes and alleys. A few battered cars were parked like fatigued beetles, hunched and lopsided. We stopped outside a dreary concrete block rising up seven floors, expressionless and anonymous. A key opened the peeling door. He took my bag—an unexpected act of courtesy, and I followed him as we climbed the six stinking flights of concrete steps, smelling of urine, tobacco, and boiled cabbage, all blending together and churning my stomach, till I thought I would add to it. I was heaving and retching by the time we reached the top, and another key let us into the apartment.

"Kusa? 'Zat you?" came a querulous voice. Well, at least he hadn't lied about his name.

A head-scarfed old woman, as ancient as the days, sat in a corner, rocking to and fro, muttering to herself. She was bundled into a heavy winter coat, even though the room was stifling hot from a cast-iron stove in the corner. "When are we going home, Kusa?"

"In a while," he replied. "But see here—this is Nina. She's come to look after you."

"Where's Dushka? I want Dushka. She promised to take me home."

"Dushka's gone. Now you have Nina." He pushed me closer.

"Nina? Have you come to take me home, dear?" The old woman looked up with pleading eyes. "I've got my bag packed. We can walk to the bus station and get the bus to Teteven." She struggled to her feet, and clasped her shabby bag of belongings.

I backed away, unsure what to do.

Kusa gently pressed the old lady back into her chair. "No, Grandmother. You're not going home today." He then turned his head and muttered to me over his shoulder, "You see? She's . . . you know . . . soft in the head. She hasn't lived in her village for ten years. But she's forgotten everything, except her home village. Take care of her, and you get board and lodging for free."

"Who's Dushka?" I asked.

"Another girl. She left. Look, I always need someone to take care of my grandmother, right? They come and go. You'll go, too. But meanwhile, this is the deal if you want a roof over your head. You watch her. She's always trying to get out the door and go to the bus station. Keep it locked when you're in, and when you're out."

"Where do I sleep?"

"Behind that curtain with her. I sleep here on the sofa—when I'm home. I have business to do. It takes me away—sometimes for days. That's why I need you. If you don't want to stay—there's the door."

"I'll stay," I whispered. *What was the choice?*

"There's a stove over there, and vegetables in that basket. Cook us something. I'm starving," he said with rough command.

I straightaway began preparing a meal, peeling and chopping vegetables to make a good thick broth. All the while I watched Kusa out of the corner of my eye; watched how he busied about, flicking through papers, making notes in his diary, and smoking so heavily that soon the flat was a smog of tobacco smoke, which he seemed oblivious of, even when his old grandmother began to cough and wheeze.

He straightened abruptly. "Got to make a phone call. Be back soon." As he closed the door, he called back, "Don't forget to lock it after me—even if I'm only gone five minutes." I obeyed.

He was gone more than five minutes. After an hour, when the broth was cooked, and the old lady was half dozing and muttering, I felt so starved I found two bowls and spoons and ladled out a portion for each of us. There was one small table, piled high with Kusa's papers and stuff, but I managed to clear a space and brought the old lady to sit in front of her bowl.

But she just stared into it and, despite all my encouragement, wouldn't pick up the spoon. "They'll have supper ready for me back at the village," she said. "I mustn't spoil my appetite."

"Here, just a little." I tried coaxing her, as I used to coax my little sister, Katya. "Just take a sip. It's a long way back to the village, and you'll be hungry."

After the meal, I washed up, and still there was no sign of Kusa, so I undressed the old lady as best I could and put her to bed, reassuring her that we would go to the bus station tomorrow. Finally, dead on my feet, I collapsed fully dressed onto the small camp bed next to the old lady's bed, and fell deeply asleep.

It was the old lady who awoke me at some predawn hour, begging to be escorted to the toilet, and, as I led her through the living room to the toilet out in the corridor, I saw that Kusa had returned and was rolled into a grubby sleeping bag on the sofa. He made no movement when we shuffled past, opening and shutting the door, nor when we returned; I didn't ask any questions, neither the following morning nor the next day.

And that's how life went on, with days extending into weeks. Kusa came and went. I never knew where he'd go, or how long he'd be. Sometimes it really was five minutes—down to the telephone in the bar across the street. But other times he would disappear for days, returning haggard and exhausted, and would fall onto the sofa, sometimes fully dressed, and sleep; sometimes sleeping for sixteen hours at a time. I knew about his gun. He was never without it, and he even slept with it under his pillow, but I never asked questions.

Day after day after day, I washed, fed, and cared for the old lady, who, nonetheless, every day put on her overcoat and sat by the door with her packed bag, waiting for someone to take her to the bus.

Sometimes, Kusa showed me gratitude; tenderness even. He would stroke my cheek, murmuring, "You're a good girl," and sometimes he kissed me, and I felt my insides turn over.

Kusa told me never to leave the flat alone, and not to buy anything. Kusa thought of everything, and always brought back provisions—sometimes even treats like chocolate. But there were times when I was so desperate to escape the close, fetid atmosphere that when the old woman fell into a fitful doze, I risked slipping out, locking the door behind me, just to walk the streets, gulp in the fresh air, look at the cloud-scattered sky, listen to the birds chirping, or the dogs barking—just to feel I still lived on the earth, and that there was life out there.

Once, Kusa returned unexpectedly to find me out, even though his old grandmother was still asleep and had not been aware of my absence. He beat me when I got back. He beat me so hard, my arms and face were covered in bruises, and my eyes were both black and blue. If I'd known he could turn on me like that, I would never have gone with him; never fallen in love with him. But it was too late. I knew whatever he did, I would love him.

10

THE THREE MONKEYS

When Mr. Baldwin's night duties ended at six in the morning, he would return to the flat, prepare Benny's packed lunch, and set the table for breakfast. Then he would wake up his son to get ready for school.

They would always breakfast together, sitting at the small round table in the kitchen, with its red-and-white-checkered tablecloth. Benny's dad liked a tablecloth—said it was more civilized. Anyway, Granny in Barbados had given it to him years ago. Benny stared at it now feeling sick to his stomach. He walked his fingers into the red squares, avoiding the white squares, as if somehow he could find a route out of the trouble he was heading into.

Benny didn't look up as his father came in, or respond to his hair being ruffled affectionately. "All right, son?" he grunted as he put the kettle on.

"Hmmm!" Benny grunted back. Did he know about last night?

He had hardly slept for worrying about it. He wished he'd properly seen the woman on the underground, but he was too busy keeping up with Nettie. He had jeered at Nettie for thinking she'd seen Miss Kovachev, but now he wasn't so sure; not after what he had seen last night. Not after that woman was dragged in by Don and another of Vlad's men: a woman in a purple head scarf.

Benny tried to suppress the panic rising up his gullet. Had he and Nettie been watched and followed from the moment they left home, but for some reason were not reported? Had someone hoped that he and Nettie might lead them to Miss Kovachev? What worried him the most was Nettie saying someone had pulled her back off the train. If it had been Swivel-Eyes or Ethan, then surely they would have recognized each other. They would have been reported, and his father would have got to hear about it, as well as Vlad himself. Could it have been Don? But they'd have seen him. Perhaps Nettie was wrong. In all that crowd, someone could have just jostled her?

"How yer doing, son?" His father sat down opposite him with a pot of tea and began pouring it.

"Okay, Dad," Benny replied warily, and looked up into his father's face to see if he could read whether there was going to be trouble. He shook out some cereal, braced for angry confrontation, expecting his father to demand what the hell he was doing going out last night with Nettie. This would be it. There would be trouble as he had never known before. But his father didn't say a word, and his expression didn't alter as he sliced some bread, put it in the toaster, and asked his son to pass the marmalade. Benny could hardly believe it. His father hadn't been told.

His father never gossiped about his job: who he saw, or what went on. Whatever Benny knew, he knew from prying, sneaking and creeping about the house. His father was Vlad's man—meticulously loyal and discreet. If Benny asked a question that was out of order, his father would tap his nose and say, "Remember the three monkeys." There were three brass monkeys sitting in a row on the mantelpiece, which were his mother's. One monkey covered his eyes, one his mouth, and the other his ears. "See no evil, speak no evil, hear no evil."

Benny risked saying, "What did happen to that Miss Kovachev, Dad?"

Did his father's hand tremble slightly as he paused buttering the toast? "Funny question. Why do you want to know?"

"Thought I saw her the other day, yeh, coming back from school."

"When was that, then? You didn't talk to her, did you?" His father looked startled. "You know what I've told you about . . ."

"No, Dad! I didn't. I just saw her the other day. I've never talked to her—not even when she worked here. I just wondered, that's all, 'cause she left so sudden, you know what I mean?"

"People come and go in this house," said his father, continuing his buttering with violent movements. "You know the three monkeys rule. Stick to it, son, and we'll be all right. Gettit?"

Yes, thought Benny. People come and go. At least his father didn't know about last night, but it hardly made him feel any better. Benny saw unease—or was it fear?—in his father's eyes. Perhaps it had always been there and he had never noticed it—until now.

"Why do you think she went, Dad?"

"Hey, man! Don't you ever listen to a word I say?" His father looked up, still suspicious. "Why do you want to know? She's been gone for months. What's this sudden interest in Miss Kovachev? I hope you haven't been gossiping at school?"

"No, Dad! Honest. I was only wondering."

"Well, you can keep wondering. The comings and goings in this house are none of our business, and just you remember that, my lad. This is a special house. You don't make mistakes in a house like this. All of us who live under this roof have to be loyal, one hundred and ten percent, know what I mean? You know the rule. Remember the monkeys." He tapped the side of his nose. "Break it even once, and we're out. I hope you understand that, Benny boy. I really hope you do."

"I do, Dad, honest. But you and me, we can talk to each other, yeh? I can keep secrets."

"I tell you, Benny, I don't even trust these walls to keep secrets. Maybe Miss Kovachev went because she got nosy. I'm not having you know too much. If it's one thing Mr. Roberts won't tolerate, it's gossip or any invasion of his privacy. See? I don't know everything, and don't want to. Teacher that she was, that Miss Kovachev, she didn't learn the lesson of the three monkeys. If you can't learn it either, can't keep your mouth shut, can't keep things to yourself, then you'd better go and join your mother in Barbados."

For the first time, Benny thought his dad was beginning to look old. He stooped slightly—perhaps from too much sitting in the hall; his pitch-black curly hair was beginning to edge with gray, like waves in the sea are flecked with surf. His face was kind, mostly. Benny knew his father had never let him down; was never one to shout or rage, or clip him around the ear, as he knew some other fathers did; he was always there for him—and yet—sometimes his face was like a mahogany mask, just as it was now, and Benny couldn't work out what he was thinking.

"When is Mum coming back?"

"When she can. When Granddad's better."

Benny felt an unexpected lump rise up his throat as he realized how much he missed her. "Hope it's soon," he muttered, shoving a piece of toast into his mouth.

———

"Did you go dancing last night, darling?" Nanny asked Nettie. "Is that why you're so tired? Are your shoes worn through?" She was reminding Nettie of one of her favorite fairy tales—the Twelve Dancing Princesses who crept out every night, down secret steps that led from their room into sparkling forests of diamonds, silver, and gold, until they reached a lake where a boat was waiting, to ferry them across to an island—to a ball in full swing. The princesses danced all night until, just before dawn, they crept back to their beds, their shoes completely worn through.

Nanny had had to coax her to get up. Nettie felt as though she had danced all night. She had woken exhausted, and the events of last night still chased through her head.

"Do you always tell the truth, Nanny?" asked Nettie as she dressed.

"Of course!" Nanny replied without hesitation. "The trouble with lies is that it's never just one. One lie leads to another, and then . . . but . . ." she qualified her response. "I try to tell the truth always, but everyone tells little white lies every now and then. Sometimes the truth is painful or cruel, and you have to weigh up the hurt you can cause by telling the truth on the one hand, with the lie which protects on the other. Why hurt someone unnecessarily? It may be better to tell a little lie."

"Is that why they won't tell me where Miss Kovachev has gone?"

Nanny didn't reply immediately. Finally: "I expect so. They know how attached you were to her. I don't know why she went or where—and that's the honest truth. I'm surprised you're still fretting about it. You must accept your father and mother's explanation. Please, Nettie, just accept it," she urged.

What Nettie accepted was that people told lies. Her own mother and father told lies—and even Nanny did. Now she, Nettie, was telling lies, too. Well—not directly, she argued to herself. No one knew she had gone out last night, so no one asked her where she'd been. And as no one asked her, she didn't need to lie. But she had deceived—and that was the same as lying.

It was during her morning break when her cell phone beeped. A message from Benny. CME 2 TWR RM.

When she arrived it was to find Benny slumped on the sofa in the sitting room. His face was solemn, his expression shifting, and he didn't look her in the eye.

"Benny? Something up? Aren't you going to school today?"

"I've skipped assembly. Your dad's back, yeh?"

"Don't think so. Back tomorrow, but you never know with Dad."

"No—you never know with your father," Benny repeated softly. "I nearly got spotted last night—I saw . . ." He hesitated. *Miss Kovachev.* He couldn't say it.

"Your father, you mean? Did he see you?" gasped Nettie.

"No, he didn't see me, yeh, but—" *Your father nearly did.* Benny thought it, but didn't say it out loud. "Look, Nettie, you've got to stop asking questions about Miss Kovachev."

"Why? Who said so?"

"I say so. I tried discussing it with my dad, yeh, and he wouldn't talk about it. He looked a bit—well, scared, you know what I mean? In this house, you don't talk. You keep secrets. Otherwise it's . . ." He swiped a finger across his throat. "It's what business is about, gottit? Your dad's a big businessman—and people in business have enemies and secrets."

"What's that got to do with Miss Kovachev?"

"You don't get it, do you?" He was suddenly angry. "Dad and

me—we could get kicked out, just for asking the wrong questions, just like that, yeh?" He clicked his fingers. "Or worse."

"Worse?" Nettie frowned.

"Your father, he's, well, he's powerful, Nettie. I know he's your dad an' all that, yeh? But he's powerful."

"He'd never do anything to you. I wouldn't let him," said Nettie stoutly.

"Yeh—like your Miss Kovachev! Couldn't stop her vanishing, could yer?"

Nettie hung her head. "Are you telling me my father *sent* her away?"

"No, no! I mean—I don't know. People just go, yeh."

Benny knows something. He's lying to me, too—even if they are little white lies.

"I think we may have been followed last night."

"What? No!" Her breath sucked in with horror. "We would have been stopped. Swivel-Eyes would have stopped me."

"Maybe we weren't spotted by the bodyguards. Maybe it was someone else. Don?" murmured Benny.

"Don?" Nettie shook her head in disbelief.

"I saw him after I left you. He came in through the front door just as I was leaving you last night." *See no evil, speak no evil, see no evil, speak no evil.*

"So?" Nettie was puzzled. "He's allowed to come and go, isn't he? You don't think he was following us, do you?" Nettie was aghast. "How could he? How would he know we had gone?"

"I dunno, but . . . well, maybe it was chance, yeh? Perhaps he was out, and happened to see us, and followed us, know what I mean? It fits, yeh?" argued Benny. "I just felt he was up to something.

Remember what you overheard in your study? And what about what happened on the tube? You said someone pulled you back off the train."

"And you thought I was imagining things," retorted Nettie. "But it can't have been Don. I would have seen him. I would have known."

I saw evil, I heard evil, say nothing, say nothing. "No, you're right. It couldn't have been Don," Benny agreed, but his brain raced on, grappling with his unease. What if it was one of Don's men—the one who came in with Don last night, maybe he pulled Nettie off the train. He breathed out heavily. "But . . . what if . . ." he said carefully, "what if Don has a reason for wanting to find Miss Kovachev? After all, he's got you to write your memories, maybe he was hoping you'd tell him something."

"But why, Benny? What's she done?"

"What if she's in a racket?" *See no evil, speak no evil, hear no evil.*

"Whose racket? You mean my father's? I thought you said Don was in the racket, so why would he—?"

"I dunno. It's complicated. I dunno what I'm saying. It's just that—how . . ." He stopped, full of hesitation. How could he tell Nettie what he had seen?

"Benny? I don't understand what you're saying. I don't know what my father's racket is—his business—or whatever you call it. I don't know how Miss Kovachev could be involved; she was just my teacher. And what about Don?"

"What about Don!" His voice was filled with sarcasm. "Like you said. If he'd been on the underground, you'd have seen him, yeh? So he can't have seen us. Anyway, no need for you to fret. He can't hurt you, only me and me dad. We'd both better be like the three monkeys, yeh? See no evil, speak no evil, hear no evil, know what I mean? I must go." Benny jumped up. "Got school, yeh. See yer later, Nettie." And he headed for the back stairs in the bathroom.

"But, Benny! If you're right, and Don is looking for Miss Kovachev, there must be a reason. You want to be a secret agent when you grow up, don't you?" Her voice trailed after him as he opened the bathroom cupboard and was gone.

"Just watch out for him!" His voice echoed back up the stairwell.

When Nettie returned to the schoolroom she was nervous. Don was sitting there at his table. His domelike head made him look like a stone statue in the gray light. He barely moved as she entered. Only his eyes followed her around, and his voice seemed to come from deep within. "Good morning, Nettie."

"Good morning, Don," she replied automatically, and sat down at her lonely table. She had two secrets that burned in her brain, so fiercely, and she wondered if Don would see them. Did he know that she had crept out and gone on the underground with Benny? And did he see her running after Miss Kovachev, begging her to stop? *It was her, it was her.*

Don stared into her eyes, as if probing her thoughts. She had to say to herself over and over again, *He didn't see me, he didn't see me. He can't know that I overheard him in the classroom, and he doesn't know I went on the underground last night.* But he stared so hard it was as though he was discovering everything, and that her very thoughts would give her away.

"Now we've got to know each other better," said Don, "let's try writing down memories again. I want to know how far back you can go. It's memory that makes you who you are; memory that allows you to read and write and speak. Just think, if you lost your memory, you wouldn't know who you are, where you lived, you wouldn't recognize your mother or father, me, or Nanny—and you wouldn't remember even Miss Kovachev." His voice was soft and coaxing. "I know how much you cared for Miss Kovachev. I never knew her, I'm sorry to say, but I'd really like to know what kind of person she was. Why not write about the last time you saw her?"

Nettie stared at him, and now it was his turn to look uneasy, as though somehow she was entering *his* brain and reading *his* thoughts.

"Is that a problem, Nettie?" he asked finally, as she went on staring.

"Er . . . no! No problem. I was just trying to remember, that's all." *Benny's right. Watch out for Don. He's tricking me. He's trying to find something out,* she thought, *but what?* She wrote carefully, taking fifteen minutes or so to fill up both sides of a page. She looked up. "Done," she said without any emotion.

"Hey, Nettie! That's wonderful! That's the longest bit of writing you've done for me since I came. Let me see."

Nettie took it over to him, and went back to her place. She saw the eagerness with which he read it, and saw how his expression changed from keen expectation to angry disappointment. She had written about the time Miss Kovachev had taken her to the ballet to see *Swan Lake*, and how wonderful the ballet had been. He whipped the page over and read to the end.

"Is that all?" he said.

"All? I thought you wanted me to remember Miss Kovachev, and I have; about the time we went to the ballet. It was brilliant. I've written nearly two whole sides. Isn't it any good?" she asked with wide-eyed innocence.

"Yes, yes! But quantity isn't quality," said Don, trying to mask his irritation. "You have certainly made a huge effort. Yes, a good job describing the ballet, but . . . Yes, I'm very pleased, I really am, but a good writer probes more deeply; explores feelings, asks questions, describes characters. You haven't told me very much about Miss Kovachev; when you last saw her, how she's doing . . ."

"That was the last time," interrupted Nettie.

". . . and where she is and—" He stopped, as if afraid he'd gone too far. There was an abrupt silence. Nettie stopped breathing as she listened to her heart beating, the clock ticking, the birds outside on the balcony chirruping, and a far distant boom of London traffic. Then Don was moving on to another topic. "We'd better get on to math, I suppose." She breathed again.

But she could hardly concentrate. The ballet music from *Swan Lake* kept going around and around in her head. She kept thinking of the magician in the ballet—he was a bit like Benny's story about Dracula. He liked to steal girls and keep them in his power, except instead of impaling them on spikes, or sucking their blood, he turned them into swans.

Don had asked her to remember the last time she saw Miss Kovachev; and she had written about going to see *Swan Lake* with her, but she had not remembered the most important thing. Not until now. Miss Kovachev had left that very night—the night of *Swan Lake*. How could she have forgotten that before going to bed, Miss Kovachev had kissed her goodnight and whispered, "Always be a swan, but beware of evil magicians."

Nettie looked up openmouthed—as if she held the universe in her throat. Don frowned questioningly. She shut her mouth and bent over her book, trying not to display the anguished emotions that fled across her face. *That was Miss Kovachev's goodbye.*

11

PRINCESS SWAN

Later that afternoon, Nettie went to Great-aunt Laetitia for a lesson. Great-aunt seemed not to notice her pupil's distraction. She praised her. *"Bien, bien, chérie!"* Her feet were curving beautifully, her ankles were strengthening. *"Ah, ma petite! Maintenant, tu es bien prête à faire des pointes."*

Nettie could hardly believe her ears. "Can I really get pointe shoes now?" Everything else went out of her head.

"We'll go and buy them together," said Great-aunt.

At last! How Nettie had longed to start practicing those fouettés, going up and down *en pointe* while pirouetting, so that one day she could dance like the black swan, Odile, enchanting the prince by whirling around and around doing the thirty-two fouettés all in one go.

After the technical class, Great-aunt asked Mara to play music from *Swan Lake*, and Nettie danced. She danced, imagining she was Odette, transformed into a tragic white swan. She danced with body and soul, to make up for her deception of last night—trying to redeem herself, but also with a kind of sadness; a yearning for freedom. She remembered her dream of last night, of Miss Kovachev running along the riverbank being pursued by a terrible cloaked figure.

"*Ma petite?*" Great-aunt cupped the young girl's face in her ancient hand. "*Aujourd'hui, tu danses avec un esprit tragique et merveilleux.* Today, you are dancing with a tragic and marvelous spirit. *Tu vas bien? Tu n'es pas malade?* You're not ill?"

"No, no, Aunt, just bad dreams. I was wondering about Odile. Her father was an evil magician, so is that why she, too, was bad?"

"Ah! The sins of the father," sighed Great-aunt, moving away in a graceful swoop.

"There are many bad magicians in this world, and poor girls who are trapped like swans," cried Mara from her place at the piano.

"Enough gloom, Mara!" snapped Great-aunt. "We must have something more cheerful. Play a tarantella!"

It was a strenuous dance. "Lift, lift. Lift! Raise your knees higher—waist high!" shrieked Great-aunt, and Nettie was panting when it was over.

"*Pas mal, ma chérie,* not bad. Soon you must go to ballet school. It is necessary to dance with others; dance with the boys."

"Oh, school! I'd love to go. Did you go to school when you were a girl, Aunt? I mean proper school?"

"School? Good gracious no. *La danse!* Dancing—*c'était ma vie!* It was my life."

"So who taught you to read and write?" asked Nettie. "Did you have a tutor, like Miss Kovachev, or Don?"

"Pah! I forget." The ancient woman frowned. "Perhaps I went to school for a bit, but very quickly I was doing nothing but dancing. I joined a company when I was fourteen."

"I went to school till I was fourteen," chortled old Mara from her seat at the piano. "I was a wicked, naughty girl; always getting into trouble; always playing the piano instead of studying my lessons. But I had a living to earn, too. Fate brought me to Madame." And she bowed her head with respect and admiration before the aged prima donna.

"Perhaps I could go to school," murmured Nettie. "I'd really like to. Mama says no."

Great-aunt grunted through tight lips, and frowned. "That is the way things are in this house," she muttered. "You cannot choose the family you are born into, but you can choose what becomes of you." The lights went off. There was a gasp! The lights came on again—off again—and on again.

"He's back! The boy's back," Mara whispered with glee.

"It's only B—" Nettie nearly gave him away

She thought Great-aunt would be angry, but instead the old lady smiled dreamily. "He's come again; another visitation from the other side!"

"He's been so naughty! *Très, très, très méchant.*" Mara wagged her finger and chortled with delight. "He took my hair curlers and put them inside the piano. *Quelle sottise!* What wickedness! It made such a funny sound, even Madame laughed. See how it pleases her? Oh, you children are a joy—the one from the other side, and you."

Nettie laughed, too, as a fleeting shadow slid through the door. Benny was back. She had lots to tell him. Her face became sober as she continued dancing. Mara played throbbing tunes which transported her to a dark forest with a lake, and there, like the prince, she hid, waiting for sunset, when the flock of swans would return and emerge from the lake to be human between midnight and dawn. The music came to the violin solo, in the bit where the swan princess, Odette, and Siegfried, the prince, fall in love. As she danced, she imagined that Miss Kovachev had been captured by an evil magician and turned into a swan. Nettie felt a prisoner, too, and the only way she could begin to escape was to go to school like Benny.

When ballet class was over, she sent Benny a text.

U R RITE ABT DON.

"I want to go to school, please!"

A few days later, Nettie and her mother were on their way to Frith-wood, to see the new gelding. Nettie brought up the subject of school. Sitting in the back of the BMW with her mother, she said, "There's one near Regent's Park," remembering what Benny had told her. "I've seen the children down the road. They all go. Please, Mama."

Peachy threw back her pretty face, with all her fiery hair falling back, showing her neat ears glinting with diamond earrings. "I've never heard of a child wanting to go to school." She smiled. "Why, darling, you have a teacher all to yourself, and when we go away, Don will come, too. If you were at school, you couldn't just sail with us on *Betsy May* to the Bahamas, or fly to the villa in Tuscany—and you know how much you love it there. Besides . . ." She paused, and sat up straight, her face becoming serious, as though there was another reason.

Nettie waited expectantly for her mother to finish the sentence, but she didn't. "I could walk there—or take the tube. I'd really like that," Nettie suggested.

"No, no, no! The point is, my darling"—Peachy seemed to change her mind about saying what she was going to say—"we'd hate to leave you behind when we go away, and besides, you get a far better education being with us, visiting places all around the world instead of reading about them in dreary old books. I can't imagine why you're so keen."

"I want friends; real friends. Not just your friends' kids."

"You have Marie-Claire and Carmen and the Hauser twins and dear little Alice!"

"I didn't choose them. They're not *my* friends. I want my own. Why am I different? Even princesses go to school."

"They have round-the-clock protection," her mother said.

"So do we," retorted Nettie, glancing through the rear window and glimpsing Swivel-Eyes on his motorbike. "Tamas could come with me."

"Honey, you're being a real pain today. What's got into you?"

"I just think I'd like to go to school." Nettie frowned.

"Well the answer's no. No, no, no! We don't think it's the right thing for you." And Peachy cataloged more reasons why school was out of the question: how Nettie would hate it; how all children hate school, she was sure.

Nettie wanted to say, "Benny doesn't hate school." But he was a secret.

"I'm going to ask Daddy if I can go to school," she said defiantly.

"By all means, but I know he'll say the same. Look, if you don't like Don, we'll find someone else. I'll talk to your father when he gets back. Oh, I can't wait to see this gelding. He sounds like a real champion." And Mother changed the subject.

While Nettie was galloping across the downs trying out her new pony, Benny was glued to the computer. Nettie's last text—U R RITE ABT DON—niggled in his brain. He opened his exercise book, where he had jotted down all of Tommy's notes.

Tommy was right. Don seemed as impregnable as Fort Knox, constantly changing his antiviral software and passwords. "Get into their minds, Benny Boy," Tommy Tinker had said. "When all else fails, it's finding their human weakness: the attention lapse, the password written down on a scrap of paper, the e-mail sent to some spyware or other. Persevere! That's your motto."

Benny persevered. It had taken him ages to work out Don's password, as he kept changing it. Every time Benny got there, it was changed again. It was almost as a mindless doodle that day, when he began playing with an anagram of Regent Mansion and a combination of numbers from Don's age and date of birth. Don had been in the army once—he knew that. But it still seemed like a miracle when, almost at random, he tapped in "Sergeant35," and up came Don's home page.

"Bingo!"

An excitement he'd never known before tightened his chest. An hour passed and then two, as Benny trawled through Don's files: his transactions, deals, contracts, and e-mails. He was in the racket all right. Benny spooled back and back—a year back; before Don came to the house as a tutor, and way before Miss Kovachev came to the house. Nothing unusual caught his eye until . . . He stopped and blinked . . . It was an e-mail sent to Vlad Roberts: "Found ideal tutor. Suggest we set a date for interview. Don."

"Look what I've got for you, Nettie!" Vlad had joined Peachy and Nettie for a TV dinner when they got back from Frithwood.

They were huddled affectionately together—Nettie enfolded into the arms of her mother and father on the huge, deep comfy sofa. He reached for a beautifully wrapped box, bound with ribbon, and plonked it on his daughter's lap. "For you, my sweet, from Russia, with love!"

She undid the ribbon around her gift box. It was a large wooden painted Russian doll with shining rosy cheeks, a bright blue blouse, a white-and-red-spotted skirt, and a red apron. "What a beauty!"

"It's a ten-set doll." Dad smiled. "Go on, open her up."

"Look what you do," cried her mother, reaching for it. She

twisted the doll at its waist and pulled it apart. "They're nesting dolls." Standing there was another doll, exactly the same. Nettie twisted her apart, too, and out came another and another with each twist, until she had ten identical dolls standing in a row from the largest to the smallest, which was as minuscule as a bean. Nettie gazed at them with quiet pleasure. *Funny. I feel like that sometimes, as if there are lots of me inside my body—only not all exactly the same me, but different.* She flung her arms around her father. "They're lovely, thank you! And look, Daddy! Look at my feet!" She splayed out her legs in front of her. "Great-aunt and I went and bought my first pair of pointe shoes!"

They were not like her old flat leather ballet shoes, but made of pink satin, with the pointe hardened inside with layers of paper, satin, and burlap. Nettie had insisted on stitching on the pink ribbons herself, despite Ella offering to do it, and they were successfully tied around her ankles. "Look at me!" she cried, raising herself up *en pointe* and pattering around the room. She felt so light, even though the shoes were still stiff and she would need to wear them into the shape of her feet. She lifted her arms gracefully. "I feel as light as a bird. I can fly!"

Vlad clapped fondly. "I see Great-aunt has been an influence, eh? Aren't you glad she came to live with us?"

"Oh, yes! I want to be a dancer like she was!" proclaimed Nettie.

"And there was me thinking my darling daughter would be a champion horsewoman!" exclaimed Vlad, bemused. "But I hope you like your new pony, eh? Mama told me what a cracker he is. Let's go to Frithwood tomorrow. I have a horse entered for the Cheltenham Gold Cup that I need to check out with Uncle Kory, and then I can watch you on your new pony."

"He's a real beauty," Peachy said. "Can't think why Nettie isn't wild about him. All she talks about is her dancing. You're such a funny one, darling."

"I do love him, Mama." Nettie pattered around the room trying out some wobbly pirouettes. "I'm calling him 'Rudi' after the great ballet dancer Rudolf Nureyev. Great-aunt told me about him and showed me photographs. He was like a prince."

"Horses and ballet—that's my girl!" Vlad laughed. "I think you should come to Russia with me, next time I go. We'll go to the ballet—they're the best dancers in the world—and then we can go and see those Cossacks—best horsemen in the world. See, Peachy? Ballet and horses—they do go together.

"Now, if we can all settle down, look what I've got for us." He slotted in a DVD. "It's about a horse, Nettie. Sorry, should have found one about a ballerina!"

As her father raised the remote to start the film, Nettie flopped down on the sofa and snuggled up to him. "Daddy, please can I go to school? Mama says no."

Vlad lowered the remote and glanced at his wife. "Where did that come from? We go from dancing to riding and now school?" He swung around to face Nettie, turning down his mouth in a theatrically sad way. "Oh, baby! Are you trying to get away from us? Don't you love us anymore?"

"She's been on and on about it for days now. I don't know what's got into her," grumbled her mother.

"Sweetheart, we'd worry about your safety," said her father, holding her close. "We don't like our little girl being out of our sight. You're too precious."

Her father always said "no" with such fondness, that she had to realize he was indeed saying "no."

"You're our only little kitten. We don't want to risk you going out into the big bad world. Not yet." Vlad blew into her curls and puffed hot air down her neck to make her giggle.

"I'm not your little kitten. I'm nearly grown up," Nettie heard herself protest angrily. Previously, Nettie would have succumbed obediently to their affectionate authority, but this time she wriggled out of her father's arms and stood up frowning.

"I don't see why I shouldn't go to school. School is good for you. I don't have any friends. I want to play sports—soccer and things."

"Soccer?" shrieked her mother. "Good heavens, child—and what on earth would Great-aunt have to say about that? I don't think ballet dancers play soccer."

"Don't make fun of me! I want to do a sport or act in school plays, or have friends to go out with. You treat me like a baby."

"Oh? And who's been filling my little girl's head about school?" asked her father with raised eyebrows.

"I . . . I read about school. The best books are about school and I . . . er . . . looked it up on the Internet." Nettie was lying. She blushed. *One lie leads to another,* she heard Nanny's voice. "I looked up the school down the road—King Edward's. I think I'd like it there. It's not far, and it would be better for me."

"I told her we could find another tutor as she seems to dislike Don, though I keep telling her no one is better than him. He's so qualified, with a degree from Oxford—and, Nettie, you get him all to yourself. You'd be in with the rabble if you went to school," exclaimed Mother. "Why, Vlad! She even talked of going by tube!"

"Everyone is rabble and riffraff to you," shouted Nettie. A wave of unexpected fury overwhelmed her. She ran out of the room, her pointes hammering across the floor, and slammed the door behind her.

12

AND WHAT OF TRUTH?

Now she knew things really had changed. She had changed. She had never been so rude and never lied. She ran not to her room but into the Round Tower, and flung herself on the bed and wept. Why? Hadn't she got the kindest, best, most wonderful parents in the world? Hadn't she got everything she wanted? New ballet shoes with pointes, a new pony, and beautiful dolls from Russia? Why was she feeling like this?

The house was filled with sighs and murmurings, as if the walls passed on whispered messages and secrets, asking themselves what was true and what was a lie. As if the hollows and spaces among the corridors and stairways, in the niches and alcoves, sympathized with the emptiness she felt; as if the atrium itself had become a void in the very center of the house, as hollow as her stomach.

She went to see Great-aunt and Mara, bursting in that evening, before bed. "I want to go to school, but they won't let me," cried Nettie in despair.

"Ah!" Great-aunt sighed. "School. Yes." Great-aunt was looking her age. She sat in the bay window like a strange bird, not quite as upright as usual, her long neck projecting slightly forward, her red hair glowing in the pale daylight, like the dying embers of a fire. She was wearing a long, dark purple velvet skirt, with a high frilly blouse which clustered around her throat and wrists; a cream woolen shawl gently sheltered her shoulders. Without her makeup on, her face was like wrinkles on water—translucent, yet timeless. Her long thin bony fingers spread out across her knees as if ready to flutter into life. "And what would become of your dancing, dearest one?" she asked softly.

"I would still dance. I would still come to you. I would still practice every single day," Nettie cried passionately.

"And what of truth? What if you learned the truth?" Great-aunt's voice stirred the air almost inaudibly.

Nettie was puzzled. "What truth, Aunt?"

Mara hovered nearby, twisting her hands. "It's right that Peachy's child should go to school, Madame. Little tickly Peachy's child." Mara came and clasped Nettie around her waist, and dropped kisses on her head. "All children should go to school, and have friends, *n'est-ce pas? Notre petite enfant grandit rapidement.* She's growing up. Odette Odile, Odette Odile!" she chanted. "To dance Odette one day, you must understand Odile, the dark one. Escape the power of evil, *n'est-ce pas?*"

I don't know when I fell in love with Kusa; perhaps from the very beginning. Perhaps when I saw him sleeping like a boy, his arm across his brow, his black hair straggling onto his neck, and I dared to remove his shoes and carefully cover him with a blanket. I dreaded him finding out I was pregnant. I had tried not to believe it myself. I couldn't have that monster Robart's baby growing inside me.

It was Kusa's grandmother who gave the game away. Demented or not, she could tell a pregnant girl. "Baby, baby!" she cackled, reaching out her withered hand to stroke my stomach.

"Is it true?" asked Kusa in a hard voice.

I nodded fearfully, too choked to speak. Yes. Hatefully pregnant. "It wasn't my fault," I wailed after him as he slammed out of the door, and I wished I could die.

He didn't come back till late the next evening. When I heard the key turn in the lock I almost hid for fear of his temper, but he entered smiling, as if pleased to see me. He was tender and kind and caressed my stomach as if it were his child inside me. "How's the littl'un?" he asked, kissing me.

From then on, I was clay in his hands; I belonged to him, and would have done anything he wanted. It even made me feel tender towards the baby inside me. I couldn't believe anyone could show me such kindness. He never said he loved me, true, but I was sure he did. I made myself believe he did. Otherwise, how could I have set off on such a journey? When Kusa suggested we should go to England, I was jubilant. "England? Really? London? Then I can try and find my sister Anna!" I flung my arms around him. "Thank you, thank you."

I hardly noticed how coldly Kusa extricated himself from my clasp, and how matter-of-fact he sounded when he said we would marry and have the baby there. It would be a British citizen, and we would be able to stay forever. So he said.

For the first time in years, I felt a glorious hope, even when he went away again and didn't reappear for another three days. I almost danced around the flat, singing songs which made even his grandmother clap. London, London! I imagined finding Anna. We could all live together. I couldn't stop smiling as I cared for the old lady, and kept the flat in order. But his absences became even more frequent, and if I asked him where he had been, and did he need to be away so long, he snapped at me; told me to mind my own business. I was hurt by his attitude: *Surely, it is my business? It's about me, too, and the baby.* The next time I asked, he hit me. The old lady began wailing as I fled behind the curtain and crumpled onto my bed in shock. When I came out he'd gone.

After that, he stayed away even more. Although he hardly spoke to me now, hardly touched me, I still craved for him to return each time. I loved him so much, I felt that nothing on earth could make me stop loving him, no matter what he did to me. One day he came home, slept as always, and on awaking, said he now had the money, and had bought us a passage to England. He said everything was arranged, and all we must do is to wait for the call to come.

I rushed over to embrace him. He was suddenly tender and held me close.

"Is your grandmother coming, too?" I asked, choked with emotion.

"I'm taking her back to her village tomorrow. I found someone to look after her, and I will send them money from England."

It was all so plausible, yet doubt raged in my mind. I loved him, yet wanted to hate him. I could see how cruel he could be; I feared him, yet he could be so charming and loving that my knees turned to water. He could talk so passionately about what he wanted from life. Sometimes he made everything seem reasonable, possible, achievable; how we would get to England, have a British baby, and live happily ever after.

The call came one evening just after sundown. A message pushed beneath the door saying to be at the bus station at nine p.m. tonight. So soon. We were to take the bus to Pleven, some hours away, then walk to a nearby gas station where a truck would pick us up and drive us across Serbia into Hungary, and on to Austria, Germany, France—and then England.

It was a terrible journey, crammed into the back of a truck, picking up yet more people on the way also intent on going to England; days and days with so few stops. We barely talked to each other; each lost in our own thoughts, perhaps with fear in our hearts, and with doubt. But I thought of nothing except Kusa, glad to be huddled into his body, lulled by the beating of his heart, and the reassuring warmth of his neck. Occasionally, the truck stopped, to fill up with gas, or near deserted ditches to allow people to relieve themselves.

It was in Germany I lost Kusa.

We had just crossed the border and Kusa wandered away, lighting up a cigarette as he went. For a while, I saw the glowing stub burning through the early morning mist, then he vanished and did not reappear.

No one knew why. The driver didn't care, but herded everyone back. "You can't go yet. You can't go without Kusa!" I pleaded and cried, but they dragged me kicking and struggling back to the truck, a hand pressed over my mouth to stop my cries. *I bit that horrible hand, and my screams escaped, "Kusa, Kusa! You've can't leave without him . . ."* Then a sudden blow to the head struck me unconscious.

Nettie had been asked to join her father and mother for breakfast in the conservatory, instead of having it with Nanny as she usually did. The light poured through the glass, casting a filigree of shadows all around from the vines and plants that climbed up the sides. Two silent maids served them.

Vlad looked serious, as if there was something on his mind. For a moment her stomach clenched. Had he now heard about her escapade on the underground? Was that why she had been summoned to have breakfast with them?

"Nettie, darling," he finally said, "how would you like to go to school?"

She gave a shout of joy and, leaping up from the table, threw her arms around him.

"I can't have my little sweetie all unhappy now, can I? So Mama and I have talked it over—and with Don, too." He frowned. "Seems you haven't been doing well with him, and though I'd much rather you stayed at home, we thought we'd give it a try." He stopped frowning and smiled reassuringly. "It's an all girls' school—Green Lodge; a nice small school, with wonderful facilities for dancing and music. We thought it would suit you. We're going to check it out. If you don't like it, you can change your mind."

The appointment to visit Green Lodge was for ten o'clock, on a day that Vlad was free to go as well. It was a large Georgian house, nearly as big as theirs, which had been converted into a school. Nettie and her parents walked up a flight of stone steps to a large green front door with a shiny brass knob. But they had first to ring a bell and announce themselves through an intercom. Vlad was pleased by the security. Once inside, they had to check with the reception desk and be given passes with their names on them, which they then had to pin to their coats. They were shown to a plush, carpeted room off the hallway, with comfortable sofas and chairs, and school magazines to read while they waited. Nettie felt strangely calm. She stared at the coiling patterns of the carpet, listening to echoing footsteps on the tiled floor of the entrance hall outside, as a flurry of girls bustled by in their green uniforms trimmed with golden yellow. Some paused to stare briefly and vanished.

Mother crossed and uncrossed her legs, her nylon stockings swishing with each movement. "Are you sure you want this?"

she whispered into Nettie's ear. "It's making me nervous already."
Vlad was fidgety—he was used to keeping others waiting, not
being kept waiting himself. He got up, walked out of the waiting
room into the hallway, peered around a corner, then came back and
sat down. Finally, a very smart woman came out of an office; not too
old, not too young, her high heels clicking on the tiles, then silenced
as she reached the carpeted area. Her light brown bobbed hair was
beautifully waved with golden highlights, her clothes chic, with just
the right amount of jewelry. She looked casual but businesslike.

"Ah! Mr. and Mrs. Roberts, I presume? I'm Marian Rayment, the
head teacher. Welcome to Green Lodge." They shook hands. "And
this is Antonietta?" Miss Rayment held out her hand again.

"Nettie," said Nettie.

"I'd like to use your full name, Antonietta. It's such a pretty one.
But I'm sure your friends will call you Nettie, if that's what you prefer. Now, let me show you around."

Vlad, Peachy, and Nettie were given the tour with Miss Rayment
as their guide. They walked through the grounds with gardens, tennis courts, and a swimming pool.

"I didn't notice a soccer field," teased Peachy.

Girls' heads turned and watched them curiously as they moved
through the school building examining the classrooms, not with
row upon row of wooden desks, as Nettie had expected, but high-
tech classrooms fitted out with banks of computers. Nettie wondered nervously if she'd know what to do, but then they came to the
dance studio with a wall of mirrors and a practice barre for dance
classes, and her confidence flooded back.

"Our Nettie is a dancer," explained Vlad, when his daughter
gasped with delight.

"We're very proud of our dance," said Miss Rayment. "We put on a show every year, and some of our girls even take part in the Christmas Pantomime at the town hall."

"Oh, Daddy, I must come here, I must!" Nettie whispered.

After enthusing about the dance studio, Miss Rayment led them to the music department, which had a complete set of instruments, and finally, into the concert hall, of which she seemed hugely proud. "We do need a new grand piano, though," she sighed. "We'll be fund-raising for that."

When the tour was over and they were comfortably seated on the plush sofas in Miss Rayment's office, she said, "Now, Mr. Roberts, as I told your secretary on the phone, we don't have a vacancy at the moment, but we can make sure you're on the waiting list. I hope you still feel satisfied with what we can offer your daughter. We would certainly love to have her when we have a place."

"Ah," said Vlad. "I'm sure we can come to an agreement. I think we like it here, don't we, Peach honey? So does Nettie. She's thrilled with the dance studio." He laughed. "She kept pinching me all the way around saying, 'Please, Daddy, please let me come here.' So, as I'm a believer in making quick decisions and getting on with it, I think we'd like you to take Nettie immediately—and let me donate you a new grand piano. There's no need to go through the laborious task of fund-raising. I would see it as a thank-you in advance for having my daughter."

Miss Rayment's eyebrows shot up. Her cheeks colored. She looked embarrassed. Nettie wondered why. It was typical of Daddy; he was so sweet and kind: always ready to write a check if it helped to smooth the way; always putting his hand in his pocket for a twenty- or a fifty-pound note, to ease away those little inconveniences such as parking on a double yellow line, being stopped by the police for jumping a red light, or wanting just that particular restaurant table, which had otherwise been reserved.

"Well, I'm not sure . . . er . . . This is most generous of you, of course," she spluttered. "Perhaps we can discuss this nearer the beginning of next term, when I'll know my numbers."

"Next term?" repeated Peachy. "Oh dear, we really hoped she could start right away."

"Indeed." Vlad smiled. "Miss Rayment, we feel Nettie should not waste any more time. I don't think it matters that you're already halfway through the term. She'll need a little breaking in. You see, she's never been to school. This is entirely her idea. So we'd greatly appreciate it if you could take her right away. I think we've seen all that we want to see, and are agreed, aren't we, darlings?" He enclosed his wife and daughter in his arms. "And your school is exactly what we are looking for. Beautiful school! It's a real credit to you."

"Um . . . thank you . . . er . . . Mr. Roberts, this is not very regular . . . er . . . I um . . . I have to consult my governing body. As I say, we don't, strictly speaking, have a vacancy in her year at the moment." Miss Rayment struggled to exert her authority.

But Vlad was as charming as he was capable of being, when he wanted his own way. "Well look, by all means consult them. Today is Wednesday. We'd like Nettie to start on Monday. That gives you two days to consult. Is that enough?" He took out his checkbook. "Now, if I'm not mistaken, grand pianos don't come cheap—not the good ones anyway. How about I write you a check for fifty thousand pounds? That's what my wife's cost just about a year ago, didn't it, Peachy darling? And if your *governing body*"—he brushed aside those two words as if they were a mere detail—"really feel they can't accommodate Nettie, then obviously, you can tear up the check. Is that fair?" He wrote out the check and pushed it across her finely polished table.

A phone call came the next day to say that Nettie could start the following Monday.

That night, Nettie scuttled down the back stairs to Benny's door—having first ascertained that Mr. Baldwin was on duty at the desk in the hall. She knocked quietly but firmly.

An eye peered through the spyhole. The door opened. "It's you!" muttered Benny. "I've something to tell you. I've found—"

"They've given in!" interrupted Nettie, her eyes shining with excitement. "I'm going to school, starting on Monday at Green Lodge. Do you know it? They do dancing as well." She babbled on.

Benny looked disgusted. He had been going to tell her his latest discovery—Don's e-mail—but he felt a wave of irritation. She didn't want to hear what he was going to tell her. All she cared about now was this stupid school.

"Benny? Aren't you pleased?" Nettie was surprised at his lack of interest.

"Might have known you'd go to a school for poshies, yeh! Not for the likes of me. But of course, no mixing with the riffraff, eh?" he said sullenly.

"Don't be like that, Benny. Posh or not, it's only for girls, so you couldn't have gone anyway. But honestly, I wish I could be like you. I'd love to go to your school, and I'd love to go on the buses, and the underground, and walk, and go where I like—and not have Swivel-Eyes breathing down my neck, and all those bodyguards trailing along, but it will change. I'm working on it. And, Benny"— her eyes gleamed triumphantly—"I don't think you need to worry about anyone seeing us on the underground. Daddy would have said."

Oh yeah! thought Benny. There was a lot *Daddy* wouldn't have told her: that Don must have known Miss Kovachev before she came to Regent Mansion, that it was Don who had suggested Miss Kovachev should be Nettie's tutor, and now it was Don trying to find out what Nettie knew. But Nettie was so taken up with school, she no longer seemed to care.

Oh well, if she can't be bothered I'll keep the information to myself, he decided. "Look, Nettie! I've got homework now. See yer later. Okay?"

Her face dropped with disappointment. "Okay," she echoed glumly. He hadn't asked her in. "Why are you so moody?" But her words were addressed to a closed door.

13

PER COGNITIONEM AD LUCEM VERITATIS

Benny was wrong. Nettie hadn't stopped thinking about Miss Kovachev. She thought about her that first morning when she stepped out of Regent Mansion in her new school uniform and got into the limo to be driven to school. She felt a different person. Everything seemed different: she heard the birds more clearly, the sharp pip-pipping of a robin pierced her heart, and the confused squabbling of sparrows made her smile. She heard Miss Kovachev's voice in her head telling her to think of the world beneath her feet; an underground world, barely remembered: where fields and meadows and flowing rivers and streams of long ago had now become invisible, stifled by the heavy weight of the city. Yet the rivers still flowed under the concrete slabs and paved roads; the seeds of wildflowers and grasses still waited in suspended animation, waiting for the light of the sun to strike them. "They know how to wait—even for hundreds of years, and then, when the time comes, when the warmth of the sun will penetrate the cracks and fissures, they'll push through concrete; push through anything, just to reach light; and then they will grow, and flower, and take over, and this city will return to nature." So Miss Kovachev had said, and Nettie believed

her, and felt she, too, was a seedling deep underground, waiting to
be released by light.

Peckham pulled out of the back mews into the flow of traffic on
the main road, with Ethan sitting next to him in front, and Nettie
and Nanny in the back. They had driven out like that hundreds of
times, but today, even that seemed different. Nettie stared out of the
window with more curiosity and more intensity. Instead of being
separate from the world out there, she wanted to be a part of it, and
had to restrain an urge to jump out of the car and just lose herself in
the crowds of people streaming to work.

Curious eyes had observed her, that first morning, getting out of
the limo outside Green Lodge, followed by Nanny and Ethan. Not
even Nettie realized that Swivel-Eyes was there, too. Unnoticed, he
entered the school through the tradesman's entrance. Miss Rayment had taken on a new gardener, but didn't know it was one of
Vlad's men—an armed bodyguard.

Seeing all the girls streaming into school, Nettie had realized with
horror that every girl was carrying a schoolbag, and that she hadn't
got one. "Nanny! We forgot to get a bag." Nettie looked stricken, as
if she would burst into tears. Nanny reassured her. "Don't worry. It
won't matter. You shall have one by tomorrow."

"It will matter. I can't go to school without a bag. I've got to have
one today. You must get me one; go, Nanny, please go. I need it
now!"

Nanny sent Ethan off to buy one, and then entered the school
with Nettie to wait with her until someone came to take charge of
her.

There was the smell of floor polish and a rush of perfume from
the lilies and gardenias which were arranged in a giant vase on a

round chestnut inlaid table. Nettie felt self-conscious, as flurries of girls and teachers swept by. Waves of laughter and chatter were followed by silence, then resumed as the girls stared at her and Nanny, then hurried on.

The school motto painted in gold letters on a shield of oak over a great door into the library proclaimed *Per Cognitionem ad Lucem Veritatis*, which Miss Rayment had told her was Latin for *Through Knowledge to the Light of Truth*. Nettie liked the sound of the words, and whispered them to Nanny, and she liked them, too—especially the meaning. Nettie remembered Great-aunt had asked, "And what of truth?" But what if, in an upside-down world, the motto had said: "Through Lies to the Darkness of Truth"? Can you find truth through lying? Is truth always light? If there can be white lies, can there be dark truths? Nanny said it was better not to harm someone with truth. Is that why her mother had lied about Miss Kovachev? But who decides what is truth? Who decides when something is right or wrong. *Per Cognitionem ad Lucem Veritatis*. Nanny said, sometimes you just have to accept things as they are. Well, she would accept this motto. Truth was a nicer word than lies. It made her think of starlight—and what all living things were made of—and that somehow, there was real truth out there in the stars.

At last Miss Rayment had appeared. "Come, Antonietta!" she ordered in her high, clipped voice. Nettie hugged Nanny goodbye, suddenly clinging to her. "Will I be all right?" she whispered.

"Of course you will. And your schoolbag will be here very soon. Don't worry. You're a proper schoolgirl now," and she extricated herself gently and hurried out.

Nettie followed Miss Rayment, ascending a broad staircase to an upper corridor. They stopped outside a door, partly made of glass, through which she could see a room with four round tables, and four girls seated at each table, bent over their books. A large screen gleamed from the front displaying a map. Miss Rayment knocked and opened the door simultaneously. The teacher turned respectfully. The girls rose from their tables immediately and stood to silent attention, but all their eyes were focused on Nettie, and she blushed under their scrutiny.

"Forgive my interrupting, Miss Abbot. I've brought your new pupil."

"Welcome," said Miss Abbot as warmly as she was able, being a thin, nervous-looking woman with a pallid face, very pointy features, and straight mouse-colored hair. Kind but strict, Nettie thought.

"Girls!" Miss Rayment addressed them in a friendly yet authoritative voice. "We are so privileged to welcome Antonietta Roberts to our school. She is joining us partway through term due to family reasons. I hope you will be kind and helpful, and take her into your class in friendship. I believe this is the first time Antonietta has been to school, so things will seem very strange. I know you'll help her to learn the ropes. Thank you, Miss Abbot. Carry on!" And giving Nettie an encouraging pat on the back, she withdrew.

It could only have been in the time it takes to draw breath that sixteen pairs of eyes examined every aspect of her; as if she were some specimen they had never seen before: her face, her hair, her eyes, her figure; they took in her expression and demeanor, her uniform, her shoes. And only in the time it takes to expel a breath, ready for the next one, did Nettie appraise them, too, and wondered who would be her friend. Would it be the disheveled girl with a rosy face, framed in a mass of tight blond curls? She liked the look of the pale one, with a solemn face and bobbed straight dark brown hair; or the brown-skinned girl, with her pitch-black shoulder-length hair, who had smiled sympathetically at her; or perhaps the African girl, who reminded her of Benny, with the same impish face and daring eyes. There was a tall girl, with corn-colored hair drawn back into a bun, who seemed older than the others, and only gave her a languid glance before returning to her book. This was Daisy.

It was Daisy who was put in charge of her; the tall one; lanky, swanky Daisy, who seemed to do everything at a strolling pace; who spoke in a drawling voice; who blinked her eyes in slow motion, and who, Nettie discovered later in the dance class, even danced in a beautiful floating slow-motion kind of way. Miss Abbot placed her at Daisy's table, where a seat had been squeezed in to allow for a fifth person.

Nettie didn't expect the questions, the intrusions, the curiosity: who she was, and where she had come from—appearing so unexpectedly among them. There were whispers that a princess was joining them; no, the daughter of a millionaire, an oil mogul, an heiress, a film star.

At break the girls paired off, or swung away in threes and fours, linking arms; talking intimately, concerned in their own affairs, laughing at whispered jokes, while Daisy dutifully accompanied Nettie, or rather led her, strolling ahead in that lazy way of hers. The inquisition began.

"Where are you from, Antonietta?" she asked in her slow sleepy voice.

"Call me Nettie. Everyone does."

"Where are you from, Nettie?"

"What do you mean? I live in London, I was born in London, but we've also lived in Sicily, New York, and Paris. We've lived everywhere, but now we're back in London."

"Hmmm." Daisy didn't sound satisfied.

"Where's she from?" Another girl butted in.

"Everywhere, she says."

"I said I live in London now," protested Nettie, not liking the slight sneer she heard in Daisy's voice.

"But you don't look English," declared another. "I mean, Mei Lee is Chinese, Radha's Indian, Rosy's Scottish. So what are you?"

"I was born in London—I'm English, but . . ." Nettie struggled to think what she was. "I'm also a bit Russian, I think . . ." Then she remembered her mother had once said they had Native American blood in them, so she added with a flourish, "And I'm related to Pocahontas, too!" They were impressed with that.

It was as though she was a new fish in a huge pond, and other fish swam up inquisitively, to nudge and pry, and see what kind of creature she was.

Some had seen her arrive in the limousine. "Was that your father bringing you to school?"

"No, Nanny brought me, but Peckham drove—he's our chauffeur —and Ethan—he's one of our bodyguards. He came, too. Daddy had to go to Toronto this morning and Mama—well, she never gets up before ten o'clock . . ." Nettie's cheeks turned pink, though she didn't know why. What was so strange about that? But she saw the girls exchanging glances—especially when she mentioned Ella, her personal maid, the chauffeur, and the bodyguards.

"Really? Bodyguards? How many do you have?"

"Do you have one to yourself? Is he here?"

They looked around, mocking and laughing.

"No," murmured Nettie uncertainly, though knowing she had never ever been anywhere without one.

"Why do you need, like—a bodyguard? Are you a film star?" There was a snigger.

"No . . . we've always had them," Nettie said feebly.

"You must be ever so rich. Do they carry guns? I've heard, like, that bodyguards carry guns." There was a burst of laughter.

"Of course not," lied Nettie, knowing they did carry guns. She knew they did because Benny had told her, and as for being rich, she'd never thought about it.

Later, Nanny returned clutching her new schoolbag, and Nettie had cringed with embarrassment when everyone stared. Ethan had chosen to buy a fine leather briefcase, when all the other girls were carrying sports bags.

"Is he one of your bodyguards?"

"He works for my father," Nettie admitted.

"What does your father do?"

"He's a businessman," she replied vaguely.

"What's his business?"

Nettie couldn't answer exactly. "Lots of things: horses, companies, stocks and shares and things like that, and casinos."

"Casinos?" a voice shrieked in outrage.

Ignoring her, Nettie continued. "He goes everywhere, sometimes to Russia, Bulgaria, sometimes New York . . . He does this and that," she ended lamely. "I don't know exactly." *What* does *he do?* she thought to herself. She'd never been asked before. *He's in the racket.* Benny said that meant business like property, buying and selling. "Property," said Nettie. It seemed to satisfy them.

"And your mother?"

Mama? What did she do? Nettie was vague. She tried to explain how Peachy worked out with her special trainer every morning in her private gym, and consulted Chantal, her lifestyle guru; she shopped, often flying off to Milan, Paris, or New York, if Daddy said she could have the jet. She visited friends, had lunch parties and jaunts—as she called them—in Monaco, Liechtenstein, and went to health resorts in Switzerland or Sweden.

When Nettie asked what their mothers did, they all seemed to know exactly: they were lawyers and doctors, businesswomen in the city, directors of companies; one was an architect, another, a television executive, and some stayed at home to bring up their children.

"What kind of car was that you came in?" asked a girl.

"A Cadillac, custom-built." Nettie smiled. "Daddy loves them for family things, but uses his Aston Martin when he's on his own."

"Bit flashy for my taste," quipped a voice.

"Yes, Mama thinks so, too. She prefers her Jag. She's just bought an XJR," Nettie told them enthusiastically. "She loves sports cars!" Then her voice trailed away when she saw their raised eyebrows. What on earth did it matter what kind of car she came in? She had noticed all sorts of different cars dropping off the girls—four-by-fours and BMWs, big cars and small cars.

"What about you?" Nettie asked Daisy. "What kind of car did you come in?"

"Oh, I walk," drawled Daisy. "I only live ten minutes from school."

Someone told her that Daisy was titled, "like, an honorable," and related to the royal family in some way. *Yet she walks to school!* thought Nettie. "Do you have a bodyguard?" she asked.

"Don't be silly! I'm not *that* important." Daisy laughed.

Does she think I'm important? wondered Nettie.

"You can always tell when Miss Rayment thinks someone is important," laughed Daisy's best friend, Caroline. "We are so *privileged* to welcome Antonietta into our school . . ." She mimicked perfectly, and everyone burst out laughing. "You're not royalty, are you?"

"A foreign princess?"

"Of course not!" Nettie frowned. "And I'm not foreign."

"With a name like Antonietta? It's not exactly Anglo-Saxon, is it!" And the girls giggled uproariously.

They were laughing at her. She hated being called foreign. With sudden cold clarity, it occurred to Nettie that there was no reason why anyone should like her. This wasn't the stuff of books anymore. This was real, about real people, and these girls had known each other for a long time. They already had their own friendships and interests, and suddenly their exchanged looks and whispers, nudges, and intimate grins were like a high wall between her and them, and no one was really opening a door to let her in.

But they didn't ignore her either. They were curious, and the questions continued relentlessly: did she make her own bed? "Of course not," answered Nettie. "That's what maids are for, isn't it? That's what Ella does."

Only when they began to mimic her did she realize how high and mighty she had sounded: "Oh, Ella, would you tie my shoelaces! Ella! Come here immediately and put the toothpaste on my toothbrush!"

Nettie wanted to fall through the earth.

A girl called Vicky, with a fashionable haircut, asked, "Antonietta! Do you have, like—a brother?"

The girls sniggered.

"What are you laughing at?" protested Vicky coyly. "Look at her hair and all those curls. Look at those eyes and long dark lashes!" Nettie was encircled by girls scrutinizing her.

"If she has a brother, and he's got those eyelashes, he'll be quite a dish."

"Sorry, I don't," muttered Nettie, gulping back tears.

"Pity!" sniffed Vicky, moving away, as though Nettie now ceased to be of any interest to her.

Somehow, she got through that first day, looking forward especially to the dance class, which would be her last class. Surely then, she would be in her element?

At last, it was time for Nettie to change into her new green ballet tunic and tie the ribbons on her ballet shoes. Excited butterflies fluttered in her stomach. She couldn't wait to dance, even though she felt critical eyes on her as she took her place at the barre with the others. What were they thinking? What else would they find about her to mock?

"Have you had lessons before?" asked Daisy, standing as gracefully as a flamingo, with one leg raised on the barre.

"Yes," said Nettie. "My great-aunt teaches me."

"Oh really!" remarked Daisy, unimpressed, bending over her raised leg and touching her head to her knee. "Have you gone *en pointe* yet?"

"Yes," answered Nettie, bursting with pride. "Yes, yes."

Madame Courbet swept in. She was a middle-aged woman, but very petite, with salt-and-pepper hair drawn back into a bun, and sharp, critical eyes that would miss nothing. She stood before them in a calf-length full skirt and teaching shoes with square heels. There was no Mara to play the piano but, instead, a tape recorder. Daisy placed herself a little to the front. Nettie followed her, but was pulled back by another girl. "Only the best go to the front like Daisy, and we're meant to copy them!"

Madame Courbet briefly acknowledged Nettie, now standing in the back row, and didn't question what stage she was at. Perhaps there was something about the way Nettie stood; so concentrated; already having the poise and presence of a dancer.

They went into barre exercises, and soon Nettie was lost in her own world, hearing Great-aunt's voice in her head as she swung her legs, bent her knees, and pointed her toes. Everything Madame Courbet asked of them, Nettie could do, and though Madame occasionally adjusted her head, or checked the turnout of her thighs, she hardly spoke to her, or seemed to pay her any attention. Nettie didn't notice. Nothing mattered when she was dancing.

After the class, Nettie was untying her ribbons and putting on her shoes, when she was aware of Madame Courbet standing over her. "Where did you learn to dance?" she asked quietly.

"My great-aunt Laetitia. She used to be a dancer. She lives with us, and she taught me. Still does."

"I see," said Madame. "Laetitia—do I know her name?"

"Laetitia Gavrilova," said Nettie.

Madame Courbet took a step back. "Laetitia Gavrilova?" There was a deep sigh of revelation. "Aaah, well. Now I understand. Goodbye. See you next week."

"Laetitia Gavrilova?" echoed Daisy, overhearing. "Never heard of her."

"You wouldn't, *mon enfant*, she's of a very old generation; dancing even before your mother was born," sighed Madame Courbet.

After school, Nettie waited inside to be picked up, wishing she could run out and go home on her own. The girls noticed her waiting. "Waiting for Nanny, are we?" they teased, but thankfully it was Peckham who beckoned her from the door.

But there were more questions to endure when she got home: questions from Nanny, Peckham, Ella—every maid or manservant she passed called out, "How was school, Miss Nettie?" And of course, Peachy and Vlad, while enveloping her with hugs, asked if she'd loved her first day at school. Nettie was quiet and calm. She was not going to lose face and admit she'd hated every minute.

It barely got much better the next day or the next. Though a flurry of text messages passed between her and Benny, she made excuses not to see him. He would think she was too much of a princess if she confessed to him how much she was hating school. Instead, she texted him with little white lies: LUV SKOOL. LOTS OF FRENS. BUSY TONITE. She could almost hear his voice saying sarcastically, "What? Am I too much riffraff for you?"

At the end of her first week at school, Nettie finally went to visit Great-aunt with her ballet shoes dangling in her hand, braced to answer more questions.

"Ah! Peachy's child!" Mara came scuttling out to greet her, clasping her to her plump chest. "How was it? How was school? We have missed you!"

"Have you come to dance?" asked Great-aunt, rising from her chair, her long neck projecting slightly forward.

"Yes, please, Aunt!" Somehow, Nettie felt she could dance away all her troubles.

"The child still wants to dance, see! Even though she's going to school," exclaimed Mara, as if to contradict any qualms Great-aunt had had.

"Oh yes, Mara! Nothing would ever stop me wanting to dance; ever, ever, ever!" cried Nettie passionately.

"Then we won't lose you to soccer," said Great-aunt with a smile—she had heard what Nettie said she wanted to do if she went to school.

"They don't play soccer at Green Lodge. Just things like lacrosse and tennis." Nettie laughed.

Mara flew to the piano and began playing a dreamy waltz from *Swan Lake*. Great-aunt and Nettie moved into ballet steps, Nettie losing herself in graceful movements, imagining that she was Odette, transformed into a swan, a great ballerina, dancing under the spotlight on a vast stage.

"Whatever else you do, Nettie," said Great-aunt, coming to a stop in front of her niece, "you must carry on dancing. Every child, no matter how rich, should be able to earn their own living and stand on their own two feet."

"Or dance on your own two feet," giggled Mara.

Great-aunt had never talked like that before. No one had ever talked to her before about earning a living. She never thought of dancing as a way to earn a living. She danced for pleasure—and when she grew up she would be like her mother, wouldn't she?

Nettie frowned. "I don't think they like me. I seem to be different —but I don't know why."

"Nettie, *chérie*, you're different because no one is the same. All the girls in your school are different from each other, but because they group together, they seem to be the same. Soon, you'll be one of them. But whatever you do, don't forget you are *you*, and maybe the thing that makes you more different is that you can dance. Now, have you been practicing your battements? *Commence avec le petit battement.*"

Nettie stood in position, balanced on her right leg, with her thigh turned out, while her left leg fluttered in and out with pointed toe, before or in front of her right ankle. She had been practicing, finding time to do at least an hour after school before doing her homework. The carpets had been removed from her playroom so that she could dance on the wooden floor, and it looked more like a ballet studio with a wall of mirrors and a long practice barre, and she could now watch herself in detail: her arms and her feet, and the way she held her head, as she tried to perfect her moves and positions.

Her dedicated practice showed. *"Tout va bien, ma petite jeune cygne.* You're doing well, my little swan," said Great-aunt, her voice full of satisfaction.

Later, Nettie returned to her room, still in her leotard, and stood for a long time staring at her image in the mirrors. She tried to see herself as the girls saw her—she stood straight as a ballet dancer, her feet slightly turned out—with her honey-colored skin, pale blue-green eyes, her hair, expertly cut and bobbed to her neck, which could be drawn back under a bandanna for her dancing. She scrutinized herself: her nose was small, gently turned up at the tip, giving her a mischievous look, and her chin had the faintest cleft. She turned to the side, examining her profile; seeing her jaw rise confidently to her ears, meeting her high cheekbones. People often told her how pretty she was. One day, they would call her beautiful.

But for the moment, her eyes filled with tears. She knuckled them dry. "I won't cry." She stepped closer to her mirror image. "Am I different?" The question became a statement of fact. "I am different."

14

A Friend

Her name was Raisa; her father was Russian, but her mother was Bulgarian. She was a solitary girl; pale, almost sallow-skinned, with dark eyes and straight dark hair drawn back in a ponytail, who seemed to have no particular friend. Girls commented on her secondhand uniform, and whispered maliciously that she was an asylum-seeker, and only at school because they had given her a special scholarship. But more than that, Raisa was different from the rest; she was quieter, more serious, often reading instead of listening to loud music. Nettie noticed her reading a book written in the same language as one of Miss Kovachev's.

"Is that Bulgarian?" Nettie exclaimed. "Can you really read Bulgarian?"

"Yes. How did you know? It's a bit like Russian, which is my second language," replied the girl, amused, yet in a voice that was as English as could be.

"My tutor was from Bulgaria. She left a . . ." Nettie was going to say "notebook," but said instead, "A book. She left a book for me, but I can't read Bulgarian."

"Show it to me," said Raisa. "Bring it to school."

Images of those strange upside-down and back-to-front-looking words fluttered like leaves in Nettie's brain. Part of her wanted to show Raisa the notebook immediately, but the other part cried, *No, no!* It wasn't for Nettie to divulge its contents—not to someone she didn't know, couldn't trust. She hadn't even shown it to Benny yet. It still felt too private. It had all Miss Kovachev's personal thoughts and secrets, and she wasn't even sure it was for her eyes, even though Nettie felt Miss Kovachev had wanted to tell her something.

I hardly knew what was happening to me after that. I was crammed into the back of a truck with a dozen other people, all strangers to each other, our unwashed bodies smelling of the sweat of travel, and vomit and fear. There was barely room to sit down, though somehow we did, our bodies overlapping, our legs cramping, and all of us clutching our single suitcase of belongings. Three days must have passed, but it was all the same to us, in the windowless pitch darkness. We crossed borders where the truck stopped, sometimes for hours, ordered to be silent so as not to be discovered. It was like an anteroom to hell; to a dreadful eternity. They only opened the doors at night, occasionally near a source of water—a tap or a river. When we drank, it was like animals, gulping and choking, while also washing ourselves as best we could. But we never knew which country we were in until one night, when we were tipped out of the container, we smelled salt in the air, and heard the screech of gulls. "We must be by the sea," someone whispered. The next stop was surely England. England. But what could I possibly do in England without Kusa? How could I have my baby without Kusa? How could I love it?

Doors slid open to ram a few more people in, packing them even tighter together, and shut with a ringing slam. I cradled my belly with the baby inside. I felt hysteria thrusting up my throat, and I had to cram my fingers into my mouth to stop me screaming, "Let me out, let me out! I want to go back. I can't live without Kusa!"

The truck stood motionless—it seemed like for an eternity. We were as silent as corpses; ashen-faced, blank, unseeing; crushed together. Then the engine started up again, and there came the rocking motion of the sea. It brought a murmur of expectation. Soon the horrors we had endured would be over.

The motion of the ferry stopped. We had reached land again. The truck moved forwards and stopped; we heard voices; hands beat the side of the truck. We expected to be discovered; this was the moment when all could be lost. We had been instructed to maintain utter silence; we were used to that now. Hours went by. Nothing happened. People shuffled and shifted their agonized bodies, and tipped up their faces trying to suck in what was left of the thin stinking air. Nothing happened; some slipped into a fainting sleep, others groaned softly to each other, "Air, air!" Without warning, the door was flung open with a violent crash, and cold air overwhelmed us like a rush of water. A voice was yelling over and over, "Get out! Get out!"

Our carriers showed no sympathy. They didn't care that we had not had food or drink for two days, and were so cramped and stiff that we could barely stagger to our feet. They just dragged us out like sacks of garbage.

So there we were, sprawling onto English soil with our faces in the mud. The truck quickly backed up, turned around, and drove off very fast.

I saw figures rising up from the ground like wraiths in the white dawn mist, gathering together their scattered belongings, whispering and afraid. We had been dumped at a rest stop on a lonely country road. No one spoke; no one asked anything of another, in case, by forming a relationship, it would make it harder to act selfishly. It was everyone for himself now. We all knew that if we were caught, we would be sent to prison, or a detention camp, or straight back home.

I hadn't had the faintest idea where to go, or what to do. Soon everyone had gone, dispersing into the countryside, as a watery sun lifted itself up from the sea.

Alone, I began to walk away from the sea. I walked all day, keeping away from main roads, following tracks alongside hedgerows, furtive as a fox. Night fell, pitch-black night, brittle with frost. Diamond-hard constellations studded a leather-black sky. I thought: I'm so cold; I'm going to die.

Then appeared the two lights, heading towards me like a comet; a car. I didn't try to thumb it down, but the beams swept over me, catching me in their spotlight like a wild animal. It braked violently to a stop. The car door opened.

"Want a lift?"

I kept walking. The car cruised alongside me, the door still held open. "Nina? It's you, isn't it? Come on, get in. I'll give you a lift."

"I'll give you a lift," cried Nettie. She had met Raisa again in the cloakrooms. The girl looked agitated. She had a violin lesson after school at the Royal Academy, but had left her music at home.

"I can't get home and get to my lesson on time. I've got my exam next week." There were tears in her eyes. "I would have asked my mother to bring it, but she's ill. I've been up most of the night caring for her, that's why I forgot."

"Peckham will take you!" Nettie beamed as she thought of the solution. "We can stop off at your house, get the music, and then he can drive you on to the Royal Academy."

"But it's surely not on your route," cried Raisa, struggling to contain her hope, "is it?"

"It won't be a problem, I promise you," Nettie reassured her as Ethan appeared at the door. "Let's go."

Raisa, with her violin case in hand, followed Nettie out to the Cadillac and Ethan opened the rear door for the girls, before sliding into the passenger seat next to the driver. "Peckham," said Nettie, "my friend needs to go to her house. What's the address, Raisa?" Raisa told her, and Peckham tapped it into his satellite navigation. "And after that, we must take her to the Royal Academy of Music—where is it, Raisa?" Raisa told her, and expressed how grateful she was—so very, very grateful. At last Raisa relaxed, leaning back into the leather seat as she realized that her problem had been solved.

The car drove off, and the two girls talked to each other as naturally as if they had always been friends. Raisa talked about her music, and Nettie told her about her ballet. Raisa said she had been playing the violin and piano since she was three, and that she was only at Green Lodge because she had a music scholarship. "This woman from Immigration visited us in a detention center. She suggested it, otherwise my mother could never have afforded to send me to Green Lodge."

"And they do dancing," said Nettie. "I've never been to school before. I've always had a tutor, but I really wanted to go. I never cared before because I had a fantastic tutor, but she left, and then I had this man, Don, who was so boring, and that's what made me think school would be much better. Mama was so against it—Daddy, too, really, but I persuaded him. He's such a darling. What about your dad?" The minute she asked, Nettie wished she hadn't, as Raisa's eyes filled with tears.

"He died," she whispered. In a low, faltering voice, "That's why we came to England." Nettie listened in horror to Raisa's story; how her father had been a businessman, but got caught up in politics, and dismissed from his post. "They found an excuse to throw him into prison, where they treated him so badly, he died. The last thing my father told my mother was to try and get to England. We managed to save enough money to get a flight to London. They sent us to this detention camp. It was terrible. It was like being in prison, and they told us we shouldn't be here, and they would send us back. Weeks and months went by, and we began to think we'd be there forever. But I always had my violin. There was a piano there, and my mother and I used to play together. One day, a visitor to the center heard me practicing and said I was talented, and that they would try and find a way for us to stay. They got permission for me to apply for a music scholarship at Green Lodge. People really fought for us, and at last, they let us stay, especially when I got the scholarship. When they let us out of the center, my mother started giving piano lessons, and everything was going well, till she fell ill."

"Oh, Raisa, I'm so sorry." Nettie clasped her hand. "But at least you're safe now, and at a great school."

"I know . . ." Raisa sighed, as if she felt guilty about not being really happy. "I don't fit in, though. The girls—I can't be like them; I can't talk about things they do: the latest designer label clothes they've bought, the gigs they've been to, the parties they hold, the country weekends they go on, the ponies they ride. I'm sure I'd be happier at the public school, but then the music at Green Lodge is brilliant. Have you seen the new piano?"

By now, they had left the broad streets around Regent's Park, and driven into a shabbier district of treeless streets, rundown houses with dusty faded curtains hanging crookedly in grimy, unwashed windows. Peckham pulled up in front of a moldering building.

Ethan said to Raisa, "We'll wait here for you, miss." A group of boys with hooded anoraks and bicycles pulled up to remark on the car. They shouted at Raisa, "Hey! Miss Razorblade. What yer doing driving around in that snobby Cadillac? Robbed a bank, have you?"

Ethan heaved himself out of the car in a manner which suggested business. At the sight of his broad shoulders and the way he walked around the front of the car, standing before them with legs apart and hands clenched in front, the boys melted away. Raisa rushed up the crumbling steps and let herself in. Peckham met Nettie's gaze through the rear mirror. He spoke on his cell phone. Nettie knew that he disapproved; knew he was explaining things to Swivel-Eyes, who would have been following them on his motorbike. Raisa reappeared after a couple of minutes, her music case in hand, and tumbled breathlessly into the car. "Sorry, we live on the top floor."

"Don't you live in the whole house, then?" asked Nettie, but bit her tongue again as Raisa blushed miserably.

"In Bulgaria we lived in a big house with many rooms, before they took my father away. But here . . . I wish I wasn't at Green Lodge," she burst out. "It's too posh; it's for snooty rich girls." She stopped, aghast at what she'd said. "Oh! I don't mean you. I know you're rich, but you don't seem so snobby, I mean . . ." She stammered, full of embarrassed mortification. "You could drop me now at the nearest tube station. I can get there easily now."

"Of course not. We're taking you all the way." To ease Raisa's discomfort, Nettie asked, "Do you speak Bulgarian and English and Russian? You're so clever."

"Yes, we all learned English at school," Raisa said. "Nettie, did you say you had a Bulgarian tutor?"

"Yes, but she . . ."

"We're here, miss," said Peckham, pulling up outside the pillared portico of the Royal Academy of Music. He got out to open the door for her.

"Thank you, thank you!" Raisa clambered out, stumbling with gratitude. "See you tomorrow."

"Went away . . ." Nettie finished her sentence in a whisper, as she watched Raisa enter the music academy. Suddenly, she looked confident. Her back straightened with joyful eagerness. She looked so independent as she disappeared through the doors; so free; it was something she did on her own; and afterwards, she would go home on her own by bus or tube. At that moment, Nettie would have given up her limousine, her chauffeur, her bodyguards, and her maids—just to be free enough to do that.

"So, Nina! I'll give you a lift, I'll give you a lift." His voice reverberated in my brain . . . Still wanting to write that book? His voice flowed on like syrup. Trust me. I'm your friend. His foot depressed the accelerator. The car got up speed. The headlights carved their path through a black void; faster and faster. Snowflakes hurled themselves against the windshield, flared and died like fluttering moths in the burning headlights. This is how I, too, will die. I was of no more substance than a snowflake.

When the impact came—it was silent. Briefly, the car had seemed to fly, then tumble over and over. The stars swirled in the sky; then nothing.

I was engulfed by pain. No, no! Please. Don't torture me. I can't stand pain. But it was the baby demanding to be born; too soon, too soon! My guts twisted and clenched in agony. My hands thrashed out touching leaves and cold ground. My eyes rolled up to the night sky. A single star seemed to be bearing down on me. I could hear one long, hollering, shuddering scream and realized it was me.

"She was lying near a hedge."

I came slowly to my senses to hear a man's voice. Not the driver, not one of my own people, but another voice, speaking a soft, blurry English that I barely understood.

"I had a sheep lambing. Wouldn't have found her if I hadn't heard her scream."

Rough hands cupped my face. Perhaps I was home, back in my old village. The sound of soft lowing cows and bleating sheep drifted into my ears, and I could smell sweet straw and animals. Oh God— had I somehow come home? "Kusa!"

"I've phoned for an ambulance," said the farmer. "Don't worry, lass," I heard him say, "you'll be taken care of."

Taken care of? Strange how a term like that can sound reassuring or deadly. I had heard Kusa say he'd got to go and take care of someone, as he checked his gun and tucked it into an inside pocket. How would I be taken care of? Would I be sent home, or go to prison, or what?

I was lifted gently into the straw. Somewhere nearby, a small creature cried out.

"My baby? I had a baby. Can I see my baby?"

The farmer shook his head gently. There were tears in his eyes. He was weeping for me—a complete stranger. He carried a newborn lamb in his arms. It bleated like a child as he gently lowered it into my empty arms.

Then I fainted again. When I awoke I was in a small, white room. I was in a hospital. A policeman was waiting for me to wake up. Perhaps they would beat me, send me back, but instead he asked me questions, so many questions. "My baby, where is my baby?" I cried. Then he told me that my baby had died, there by the roadside.

I thought I would be glad to lose that monster's baby, but it was mine, too, and had become a part of me, and though it wasn't Kusa's, he had talked of it as if it were his. Now Kusa was gone, and the baby was dead. At that moment, I died, too. I no longer cared what would happen to me.

After a while, the policeman asked more questions. He looked puzzled when I babbled on about a car crashing. He said there had been no car. He thought my mind was wandering. The farmer had said he'd found me alone; no car, no driver, no signs of a crash like skid marks or crushed hedgerow. There were no marks on my body—not a single bump, bruise, or scratch.

I got agitated. Tried to get up; tried to run. Nurses came in to restrain me, and one gave me an injection. I heard their soft voices as I drifted back into unconsciousness. "Illegal immigrant," they muttered. "The traffickers probably abandoned her because she was about to have a baby. Dumped her on the coast; she was trying to get to London; must have got confused—what with the baby and the pain and trauma. The baby was a girl," they said.

"What will happen to me?" I asked before I drifted away.

"It all depends," said the policeman.

The next time I awoke it was to find a man sitting by my bedside. *Kusa!* I nearly called his name. Kusa—always my first thought on waking or before sleeping—but it wasn't Kusa. My dream was to waken every day and find him by my side, ready to join me in a new life. But my baby was dead. I was of no use to Kusa. No one needed me anymore, not even my baby. I had felt her move and kick, and instantly a great love had burst into my heart; a love I had never known. But now my baby girl was dead. Without this life inside me, and without Kusa, I felt useless, hopeless, unnecessary to anyone. I curled up into a tight ball, clutching the sheet around me like a shroud. I closed my eyes, taking refuge in the darkness of my mind.

The man by my bedside was not Kusa. At first, I didn't want him to know I was awake. I studied him through my tears and the screen of my eyelashes, then turned my face away from the stranger. Who was he? Another policeman? A doctor? But no, he hadn't looked like a doctor—he wasn't wearing a white coat. Immigration! That's where he's from. Then a terrifying thought made me gasp out loud. My eyes flew open. Was this man the driver?

The stranger leaned forward. "Ah! You're awake."

"Who are you?" His face wasn't like Kusa's, and I remembered how I loved seeing all the different facets of his character, moving across his face like shifting clouds: the certain and uncertain; cruel, kind, honest, and dishonest. This man had a smooth, polished face, like a blank sheet on which nothing seemed to have been written, or nothing, at any rate, which gave him away. He was not quite middle-aged, with blond hair cut trimly to his neck, and a longer bit smoothed over his forehead to one side. His brown eyes were nut hard, his mouth a thin line, yet which could give way into a slight smile, and he wore his suit like a man who always wore a suit.

I spoke in Bulgarian. He didn't understand.

"Do you speak English?" he asked. His voice was English; he was not the driver. "There's no need to be afraid. I'm not the police. You're in good hands. I've just come to ask you some questions."

I shook my head wearily. More questions?

"I have to ask," he said, but he asked them quietly, unthreateningly, as if to a friend; he spoke as if he cared about me. Which village had

I come from? Who had organized my trip to Britain? Who paid? Did I
have a passport?

I told him about Kusa. He listened. He asked if I had an address to
go to. Did I know anyone?

"My sister, Anna; she may be in London. I must find her. Could I
stay and look for her?" I slid back into a dark sleep. When I awoke, he
was still there, waiting patiently.

"Are you going to send me home, or to prison?"

"It depends . . ." said the man. "Look, call me Mike. I'm here to help
you, if you'll help me."

15

A Fabulous Gift

Things changed—of course they did! Gradually Nettie settled into school—especially after she and Raisa became friends. Now that the other girls had seen Raisa getting into the chauffeur-driven Cadillac, they wanted to be invited to tea at Regent Mansion, and find out how Nettie lived. She suddenly became popular and in demand. First she was invited to their houses, so that she would ask them back. She even went to Daisy's house, and Caroline's and Radha's, and was now drawn into their circle, invited into their gossip, picked for their teams in netball and lacrosse, and how they admired her dancing! Their parents seemed keen to know her, and she got invitations to join their daughters at the theatre or ballet, on excursions or even weekends. Never had she had so many people wanting to be her friend. Yet the questions kept coming, pecking and prying like birds of prey.

"Does you father play golf?" asked one parent. "Which club does he belong to?"

"Where did you get that divine jacket?" asked a mother. "Caroline's been pestering me for one like that."

"Do you ski?"

"Where do you go?"

"We like to rent a chalet each year."

"What exactly does your father do?"

Is this what it is like to have friends? Nettie wondered.

Seeing all the comings and goings, Benny sent her a complaining text. NO TME FR ME? GT NW FRENS? PROPER FRENS? AM I A FREN OR JST A SECRT?

Nettie could hear the sarcasm in Benny's voice when she read it, that sneer which Nettie hated; but it was true, she hadn't seen Benny for ages. She felt uneasy and guilty. She texted him. CM 2 RND RM 4.30

CAN'T, came the reply. C U 2MORRW.

"Glad you could spare a moment for me." Benny was scornful when, the next day, he showed up in the round room.

"I'm sorry, truly I am. Time just rushed away. There was so much to do and think about. Please, Benny, don't be cross. Want one?" She held out a pack of chewing gum.

He shrugged, opened up the offering, and flopped down in an easy chair, his long legs spread out arrogantly in front of him, his jaws working hard on the gum.

"You know what, Benny?" Nettie wanted to appease him. She curled up at the end of the round sofa nearest to him and leaned towards him, her chin resting on her hand. "School's not really what I expected." She waited for some kind of response, but he just stared up at the ceiling, chewing away. "It's not like the way you described yours, and it's certainly not like in Harry Potter or Enid Blyton books. I thought I'd be with a whole gang of friends. Well— there are gangs of friends, it's just that I don't feel they really like me. I mean, like me because I'm *me*." He didn't respond, nor look her in the eye to show he was listening. "You still like me, don't you? Or am I weird?"

"Yeh—you're weird, really weird," he replied cruelly. Seeing her almost burst into tears, he softened. "Nah! Only kidding! You're not weird, course not!" Benny finally looked at her. "You're odd, that's all."

"Why am I odd?" she persisted.

"I dunno. Just are. People like you are different. Doesn't mean you're not . . . nice or nothing. You're okay, yeh." And suddenly he grinned and then pulled a silly face, which usually made her laugh, though this time it didn't.

"But that's what I mean. Why am I different? You should hear the questions they ask me—really stupid ones—like where did I get my jeans from, or where did I get that shirt, that jacket, or my shoes. Like where are we going this summer for our holiday? Their parents are just as bad, always asking about my mother and father. They never want to know about me. Lots of girls call me their friend, you know, yet after all this time I feel I've only got two real friends, you and Raisa—at least I think she's my friend . . ."

Benny looked back up at the ceiling, chewing even faster on his gum. Funny that Nettie hadn't mentioned Miss Kovachev once, and there he was, still worried about her. Still beavering away at his codes and passwords, trying to find out where she was and what had happened to her. Now all Nettie could talk about was school, and a new friend—this Raisa.

She hoped Raisa was her friend. But though it was Raisa she found herself talking to at school, sitting next to at lunch, and walking around with at break, somehow she couldn't get Raisa to tell her any more about Bulgaria, as though she, too, had secrets.

And whenever Nettie invited her back to Regent Mansion, Raisa made excuses: her violin practice, homework, looking after the housework and shopping. "I don't have much spare time, and anyway," she said, "I don't like leaving my mother for so long. It must be hard for you to understand."

Nettie wanted to say, "Well why don't I go back to your place?" But she didn't like to. There must be a reason why Raisa didn't invite her home. She felt sad and dispirited—though she didn't give up. When Raisa took her violin exam and passed with distinction, Nettie gave her a boxed-set recording of the Russian violinist Maxim Vengerov, who Raisa couldn't stop talking about. Raisa was embarrassed by the gift, but thrilled and grateful, too. "I love Vengerov's playing!"

"Please come back to tea with me," begged Nettie. "I can get a maid sent around to look after your mother. It's only fair that you can see your friends," she argued. "Please, Raisa. Tell her you're my friend."

"She knows that." Raisa smiled. "She was really grateful to you for helping me get to my violin lesson that day. I'll ask her again."

"Ask if you can come next Sunday!" cried Nettie, thrilled that she had at last made a breakthrough, and by the next day it was agreed, though Raisa said her mother would be mortified if Nettie sent her maid around to look after her. "Please don't go to that trouble, I'll leave everything in order for her."

So Raisa entered Regent Mansion. It was like entering a dream, though she was quiet and restrained at the opulence that met her eyes. "Buckingham Palace can't be more luxurious," she breathed. They swam in the inky pool, they had tea and ate Cook's best chocolate cake up in Nettie's living room. Afterwards, they went along to say hello to Vlad and Peachy in the music room. "Raisa's a brilliant violinist! She's got a special music scholarship at Green Lodge because she's so good," cried Nettie.

"Then she must play my best violin," announced Vlad, unlocking a glass cupboard and drawing out a deep, reddish-brown violin. "A Guarnerius—one of the best!"

Nettie had never heard of a Guarnerius violin, but Raisa held the instrument in awe, as if it were a newborn baby. It was one of the most valuable and fabulous violins in the world. "I can't play this!" she exclaimed.

"I don't think you need worry," said Vlad, laughing. "It will play you."

So Raisa played; she played as if she was under a spell, drawing out the most glorious, resonating sounds. Sometimes her fingers flew up and down, other times they quivered with rubato, as she drew the bow in long phrases over the strings. When she finished, there were tears in her eyes. "I have never made such sounds in all my life," she said. "I never thought I could."

"My dear," cried Peachy warmly, "you're so talented!"

"Thank you," said Raisa shyly. "But it would be difficult to play badly on such an amazing instrument."

"True," agreed Vlad, "but although a Guarnerius plays you, I think you are equals, and it loved being played by someone as good as you. I hope you'll come again." He was at his most gallant. "I would be honored if you would play it. It will always be here for you." And bowing low, he took her hand and kissed her fingers as if she were a princess.

Raisa thanked him with all her heart, and Nettie went over and hugged her father for being so kind.

"I've an idea, Peachy." Vlad beamed over to his wife. "Why don't these girls perform for us at our party on Saturday night? Nettie could dance, and Raisa play the Guarnerius. You can invite your school friends, too, Nettie."

Nettie was thrilled. She had often danced little party pieces to make her father's guests smile and say complimentary things, but to do something with a friend filled her with excitement. "You will, won't you?"

Raisa nodded, though she looked terrified.

"I know what you should play," Nettie whispered. "The violin solo in *Swan Lake*, and I can dance to it. Come, I must introduce you to Great-aunt. She must hear you play it on the Guarnerius, and perhaps I can dance *en pointe*!"

Nettie, life is nothing but choices. For every one thing you choose to do, there is another choice you could have made. Now someone was putting a choice before me. The man who called himself "Mike" came to see me in the hospital again a day or two later. "Did you think it over?" he asked, pulling up a chair.

Day by day I had begun to feel better and stronger. The hospital treated me kindly, but there was always a policeman out in the corridor. Guarding me? I supposed so. After all, I was an illegal immigrant, and they didn't want me wandering off. Had I thought it over? I had done nothing but think.

I thought about my choices and feelings. I battled with my longings: I was desperately homesick now, and I was frantic to see Kusa again.

Mike said Kusa had been paid to procure me to work illegally in

London. He hadn't told anyone I was pregnant, but kept his options open for the right moment; then, before they found out, he'd walked away with the money. After all, it wasn't his baby, but that monster's. He couldn't care less. He'd been paid to do a job, and done it. Now he was luring other girls into the trap. *Forget Kusa. Think of Anna.*

"Listen," Mike said, "you can help me to stop this evil traffic."

He said he'd been doing some homework on me—ever since they picked me up. Mike had his contacts, too. Other girls had come from that area before me. "Anna—did you come across Anna?" I cried desperately. But he hadn't. "We had a card from her, then nothing. It's been over two years. Kusa said we could find her. Can we?"

"First things first," said Mike quietly. "Let's start with your village, and this man Robart."

Mike is like the driver. He knows all about me. I keep dreaming it. I'm walking along that icy road, and a car comes out of the night—its headlights flaring like the nostrils of a terrible beast, and it slows down, keeping pace with me. The door opens. I cannot see his face. I cannot see who it is, and he says, "Nina, want a lift?"

"Your landlord, wasn't he?" said Mike.

I nodded. "And Kusa?" I asked, my tears springing from my eyes.

"This man Kusa worked for your landlord, Charles Robart. Robart blackmailed your uncle Tony into paying the money to get you to England, and arranged for Kusa to pick you up at the bus station. But your landlord is small fry; he's nothing compared to his brother, Vlad Robart, in London. This brother of his started small; supplying unscrupulous employers with illegal workers, a kind of slave labor trafficked in from all over Europe. But that wasn't enough for him. Through terror, extortion, and murder even, he's become head of an organized crime syndicate, and it's him we're after. So far we haven't been able to touch him. He's clever. He lets others take the rap—this crime lord, who's grown fat and rich on all this misery, who's sitting smug and safe on a lily pad at the heart of the community, feeling untouchable. He's out there, Nina, dealing in trafficked girls, money-laundering, drugs—you name it, he's got a finger in it somewhere—yet so far, he's getting away with it. Anna went through his hands, poor girl. Do you know what hell these girls suffer? Do you know the terror, the beatings, the hopelessness? Innocent girls who thought they had come to work in a café or hotel, who find they are nothing but chattels, for men to buy and sell among themselves; girls stripped of their passports, money, who can't speak English—not even enough to ask for help; girls who die. They die, Nina; die from drug abuse; die from loss of hope, and shame; die because they are no longer useful."

Mike paused, watching the words sink into my brain as I lay back weeping.

"You can help me do something about it—catch this man, stop this trade. Save girls like you and Anna. Men like Kusa are nothing—only in it for the money. But you, Nina, and girls like you and Anna—you were never going to get paid. You were victims like flies in a spider's web. Look here"—he leaned closer, persuasively—"you could do something—help me; I wouldn't put you in danger, but it's the small pieces of information that add up and make the bigger picture." He handed me a handkerchief to blow my nose and soak up my tears. "There's no future for you back in your village. There wasn't much future for you there anyway. You're a bright woman; intelligent. You ought to be at university. I can make that happen. Your English is already quite good, but I want you to go to a language school, so that you can learn even more, and in exchange, all I want you to do is to keep your eyes and ears open. Listen to the gossip. Note down every-thing—even the most trivial. You'll be offered drugs, shown ways of making money on the side—perhaps as a courier; I want to know names, places, times. I'll want to know who approaches you, what stuff they offer you, where they get it from. I want to know if you hear of gang leaders looking for labor. Some of those students will be illegals, like you; desperate for money; getting caught up with gang leaders. Anything you hear, jot it down. The smallest thing can fit like a piece of a jigsaw, and might give us the evidence we need on Vlad. He's the one we're after. Then we'll find out what happened to Anna. Help us get him, Nina, and help yourself, too. Get a degree, a job, and you'll be able to stay here; start a new life. I'll help you."

Mike went away again, and said he'd return tomorrow. Give me time to think it over.

"Find Anna? Yes, yes, yes."

16

FINDING MISS KOVACHEV

I thought you wanted to be a secret agent when you grew up." Nettie's words echoed in his brain; they seemed to taunt him. Now that she had decided she preferred dancing to being Point 007, she seemed to have stopped thinking about it; Benny would swear that she'd even forgotten about Miss Kovachev—she was so taken up with school and ballet. But for him, finding Miss Kovachev had become an obsession. Benny was desperate to prove to himself that he had the makings of a secret agent.

It wasn't just to find Miss Kovachev; it was more than that. He'd learned so much from his hacking. Vlad's racket was far bigger than he'd imagined. It frightened him. Now he knew why his father kept to the rule of the three monkeys. Benny pondered on his amazing discovery—that it was Don who had brought Miss Kovachev into the household, but that neither Don nor Vlad had known she was going to leave. Something made her run away.

All the other e-mails Benny hacked into between Swivel-Eyes, Peckham, and Ethan suggested that they were all worried she knew too much and could endanger everyone. Vlad wanted to know what, if anything, Nettie knew about Miss Kovachev's whereabouts. He was on a rampage. He wanted Miss Kovachev found, or someone would get impaled for it, and that's what Nettie had overheard Don saying.

The woman they saw on the underground had been captured by one of Vlad's men working with Don. He must be the one who pulled Nettie back. He must be the man Benny saw with Don, when they dragged the woman into the house half-drugged. He'd seen it. They'd got her, and Don must know where she was. Nettie could be right; the woman could be Miss Kovachev.

Benny told his father he wasn't feeling well. He had spent hours in front of the screen, and his head ached with all the numbers and figures he'd been playing with. He felt close to a breakthrough, so he begged a day off school.

Mr. Baldwin had agreed reluctantly. His son was looking tense and his eyes were red-rimmed. "You spend too much time in front of that computer of yours," he complained. "I'll let you stay back today, but don't make it a habit, do ya hear? And don't you disturb my beauty sleep. I've had a night of it, I can tell you."

With his father in bed, Benny went to his room, shut the door, and opened up the computer. He would never have got into other people's computers if Tommy Tinker hadn't shown him how to use back-door programs, and break in remotely. He would break into his father's computer. The first bit was easy—he'd learned his father's password ages ago. The page opened up; he got into his files—the day-to-day ones, like the car log. He knew that every time the car was used, his father recorded it in the computer. Vlad was fanatical about knowing where everyone was at all times. If this woman, whoever she was, had been taken anywhere by car that night, there would surely be an entry.

He scrolled down through the month till he came to the right day and time. Nothing. Why hadn't his father entered it? Perhaps Peckham had logged it in, but there was nothing. Benny sighed. That left Don. Don was well protected with a stiff antivirus program. How he wished Tommy Tinker was around to help him. He spooled again through Don's e-mails, checking for a date on or after he and Nettie had gone on the underground. Benny must have been goggle-eyed with fatigue, otherwise he wouldn't have missed it over and over again, spooling through, back and forth. It was the letter *K* in the subject bar that finally halted him. Don had sent an e-mail to Angel that very night.

"Angel?" Benny muttered wearily. Oh, *Angel*—Father Gabriel! The message said, "K at VR." What was VR? A further careful line-by-line search failed to give him the answer.

Benny sighed. Vlad wasn't the only one not to trust technology. He remembered the logbook—a handwritten logbook his father kept in a shelf under the desk. He should have looked there first.

Benny knew—this time with certainty—that Vlad and Peachy were away. They had flown to Marseilles in their private jet—Vlad as pilot, something he liked to keep his hand in with. With Nettie at school now, there were fewer people around. Nanny had gone off to meet a friend, Ella had a day off, and Nettie's bodyguard was in the vicinity of the school; the others who hadn't gone with Vlad were playing billiards. His father was sleeping off his night duty.

Benny let himself silently out of the flat, and went up the back stairs to the ground floor. The back door opened into the hall in an alcove opposite the main staircase where the day doorman, Dave Fox—"Foxy"—was sitting at the same desk at which Benny's father sat by night. Behind the desk was an alcove covered by a long thick Flemish tapestry which fell from ceiling to floor. Benny often sneaked behind it unbeknownst even to his father.

He opened the back-stairs door a fraction and peered out. Foxy was reading the paper in front of the flickering security screens. Gimley came by. "Hey, Foxy! Did you know it's Mrs. Bainbridge's birthday today? Cook's made a special cake, they're just cutting it now to have with their coffee. Get along! You don't want to miss out on that. I'll join you." And the two men went down the service stairs to the kitchen. Benny grinned to himself: "Dad would never have done such a thing." Even with Vlad away, leaving the desk unattended was unthinkable. He was a stickler for duty.

Benny saw his own image flicker across the screens as he dashed across the lobby to the desk. Benny knew where the log was kept. He'd seen his father write in it so often. He eased open the drawer and pulled out the thick logbook, then crawled behind the tapestry to examine it by flashlight. He flicked the pages to the night of the underground. Nothing. He grunted with frustration. Someone must have made a note of it. He crawled back and riffled through the desk; papers, notes, instructions, but no log of the journey done that night.

He felt sick. Perhaps he really was ill. He got back to his room and lay on his bed. He shut his eyes, falling into an exhausted half sleep. Images of what he had seen that night on the underground floated across his brain. His eyes flew open. An image came back to him which he'd almost forgotten, and disregarded—his father returning to his desk and, before he took out his bag of toffees, scribbling something down on a piece of paper and putting it in his pocket.

He leaped to his feet, his energy surging back. Dad had worn the same jacket last night. It was probably draped over a chair in his bedroom. Benny thought of an excuse for being in his father's bedroom if he woke up, and then silently let himself in.

His memory was right. It took barely a few seconds for him to feel through the pockets of his father's jacket before he drew out a piece of envelope. Scribbled in pencil was: *April 6th BMW 23.45 to VR Imports, 46 Conway. Mileage: 6.6 miles. Time returned, 02.07 hours.* Bingo! Benny copied the address to his cell phone and returned the envelope to the jacket pocket.

"Conway." Back in front of his computer, Benny opened his browser and trawled through Streetmap's search results. There were so many Conways in London: Conway Gardens, Grove, Road, and Street. He focused on the only one—Conway Gardens—within an eight-mile radius, and it was between Paddington and Willesden. "Gottit," he muttered. The distance, and time taken, seemed right.

He wrote a note for his father—just in case he awoke early—and propped it by his bed. *Felt better. Gone to school. Soccer match this pm. See yer later.* He thrust his arms into his school blazer and let himself out of the flat.

A fifteen-minute bus ride brought him into the right area. He checked his notes with the directions: walk down High Street, turn left and first right into Conway Gardens.

It was a grubby street, full of rundown houses converted into endless small bedsits, and a row of shops: a newsstand, a grocery store, a clothes shop displaying in its dusty windows the kind of clothes it was impossible to imagine anyone wearing. Discarded takeout cartons rolled like tumbleweeds down the gutter. An elderly man shuffled along, head down, a newspaper clutched in his hand. Benny nearly passed a shabby door welded in between a clothing outlet and a real estate office. Number 46.

A grubby brass plate said VR IMPORT EXPORT. VR—*Vladimir Roberts, my dear Watson,* thought Benny smugly. He pushed at the door. It was locked. There was a row of bells and an intercom. He looked upwards, taking in its unpainted and neglected frontage. The building rose four stories, its windows opaque with dust and ill-hung curtains. There was nothing to indicate what was imported and exported. A blurry image at an upstairs window, perhaps a face, made him walk quickly away. It began to rain, and he took refuge in the corner newsstand, buying a bar of chocolate, then staring at the door of Number 46, wondering what was inside.

Through the clutter in the shop window, he saw a car trundle down the street and park outside the premises. A man got out. It wasn't anyone Benny knew. The passenger door opened, and another man emerged. He knew him, all right—Don.

"Sssssugar!" hissed Benny, stepping away from the window among the magazine racks. He felt a shudder of anxiety. Was this coincidence, or did they know that he had come here? Don looked around. He walked a few steps towards the newsstand. Benny shrank farther back—but there would be nowhere to hide if Don came in.

"Do you want anything more?" asked the shopkeeper suspiciously.

"Sorry. Er . . . no . . . it's just . . ." Then he saw Don whirl on his heel, produce a key from his pocket and open the door of Number 46, and the two men entered.

Benny didn't think, didn't think. He could see the door of VR closing slowly by itself, on one of those springs, and instinctively dashed out of the newsstand and thrust his hand forward to stop it before it locked itself. Holding the door ajar on the palm of his hand, he slipped inside, and went limp with shock. Don and his companion were only halfway up a narrow, bare flight of stairs. The door slid from his hand to shut behind him with a click. He was done for. But it was the sound they would have expected to hear, so they didn't turn around. Benny stared at the figures as they plodded to the top and carried on without looking back. Through the pounding of blood in his head, he heard their footsteps continue climbing to the next flight and the next. A door opened and closed in the distance above his head. He hadn't realized that he had stopped breathing until he gasped with relief.

There was a button in the wall to put on a light, but he didn't push it. *Now what?* He stared into the gloom. He was either going to climb those stairs or get out.

Voices drifted down to him from somewhere above. He began to ascend, very softly, looking for a means of escape if they should come down. A door on the first landing led to a lavatory. He noted it. Two other doors were shut. He pressed his ear to them, but heard nothing. He climbed to the next floor. A similar layout: a lavatory and two other rooms with their doors closed. The voices were closer now, coming from the third floor, men's voices, interspersed with a woman's hoarse, worn-out voice, pleading, "I don't know anything. Nothing, I tell you. Don't hurt me. I just taught the child."

A single long thin scream echoed through the building.

I had made up my mind. I could see my future now, in a way I had never been able to see it before. When Mike returned the next day, I said yes, I would help him.

Mike told me I was going to find Anna, and help defeat people like Robart and Kusa. When I was discharged from the hospital, Mike took me first to a small hotel in Paddington where I was to stay till he'd sorted things out. He gave me some money to buy clothes, food, and toiletries. One day he came and told me I had been enrolled in a language school just outside London. "We think many girls have been picked up here and taken to work for Robart." I would start the following week.

He showed me photographs of girls who had been lured to England with the promise of jobs and the good life, only to find themselves stripped of everything and become slaves. They were forced into a secret world, invisible, working twelve-hour days on fruit farms and in fish distribution centers; or worse, being forced into prostitution and drug dealing. All the time I thought of Anna. Had this happened to her? Had she lived like this? Crammed into pitiful rooms; threatened and abused. Unable to speak English, they hadn't been able to communicate with the outside world and, anyway, were too terrified to try, and too ashamed to tell their families. I cried when I saw their bodies, battered and bruised, thin and emaciated, racked from drugs and abuse. They were the most miserable creatures I had ever seen. I couldn't bear to think this had been Anna's fate, and could have been mine.

Mike told me I must be like other students—live in a student hostel, lead a student life, and see what materialized. I must appear to be newly arrived, uncertain. He said I must go with my instincts, but he would want to know who my friends were, and who befriended me; who might see me as a possible victim. He said, "Less is more; seem less bright, less capable," and that I would learn more if I was not too clever. "We want them to know you're Bulgarian. Take yourself back to that winter's night, walking along the road. Pick up from where you left off. You are an illegal immigrant; be fearful, be ignorant. Do you understand?"

He gave me a bankbook and told me that a regular amount would be paid into it which I could draw for myself. It wasn't a lot, but enough to get by. If I didn't have too much money, he said, I'd find out what forced some girls to try and earn extra. Then he gave me the address of the language college. I was to find it for myself.

Mike said if we were lucky, I would break into their network. "You'll report to me once a month," he instructed. "But never e-mail." He gave me a cell phone. "Text is safer—you can't be overheard." But I was only to contact him in an emergency—if I was in trouble. He would contact me.

"This is all I want from you, Nina."

All? At first I was so fearful, especially those early days when I enrolled at the school, and had to fill in lots of forms. But soon I became more confident and began to settle in. You see, Nettie, I had been trained well, by Mike. I didn't need to pretend I was short of money—some days I hadn't enough to eat. It wasn't long before the drug dealers made contact, and I was soon buying and selling the stuff. Once a month, Mike would text and make an arrangement to meet. I would hand over all my notes.

Then I met Don. He was a tutor at the college. He was quite friendly with the students—especially the females. It was Don who introduced me to someone who needed a translator for some Bulgarian girls—newly arrived—and I knew I was getting closer to the people traffickers. I recognized the type immediately: girls like me—like Anna—girls full of hope and enthusiasm. I had to watch that enthusiasm killed as, gradually, they were drawn into the net. I had to behave despicably, cruelly, in a hard-hearted way. How they cried and begged me to help them. Oh God, forgive me. I would have given up if Mike hadn't made me remember Anna. "You're looking for Anna, don't forget. She's the one who matters." He was right. I was doing this for her. Anyone I met, I always asked if they could remember a girl called Anna. Then one day, I was approached for drugs by a young woman; she wouldn't live long—her addiction had wrecked her body. She had known Anna. For a while, they had lived together on the streets trying to raise enough money to feed their addiction. Anna, she told me, was dead. She'd died a year ago.

Anna! My sister—my darling sister. I was tormented imagining her suffering. I wanted to give up—to die, too. I couldn't help seeing those images Mike had shown me of girls curled up, dying in empty bedsits, with syringes still in their hands. "Send me home, Mike," I begged. "I don't want to be here anymore."

Once again, Mike focused my rage and grief; told me I had to find the people who did this to Anna. Not the little people, but the big ones; the ones who always got away with it; the crime lord, the blood-sucking Dracula who was the cause of all this evil.

One day Don approached me after classes. He invited me out; we went to nightclubs; he plied me with drugs; he wormed his way into my life, so that I would feel dependent on him. Do you believe in heaven, Nettie? I do know there is a hell, and that it is here on this earth, and we are all a part of it. How I loathed this man, but Mike told me to stick with him. He was excited and praised me. He had done some checking. How does a man on a part-time teacher's salary afford a six-bedroom house in Hampstead and drive a BMW convertible? "This could be our breakthrough," he said. "I want to know more. Do as he says."

Not long after, Don said he had found the perfect job for me. He said he liked me, and wanted to see me living better. A wealthy multicorporate multimillionaire businessman needed a tutor for his young daughter; someone he could trust. I accepted.

A door opened above Benny's head, and the voices were louder. "Best thing is to sell her on. She's no use to us now. Get her out of the country. Use the Thai connection." They were coming down.

No time to dash for the lavatory. Benny saw a door to his right. He took a chance and turned the knob. It opened. Again, that could have been the end of him; the room could have been inhabited, but it was empty. And he slipped inside. Footsteps clattered down; he pulled the door to, softly does it; they carried on past, as if in a hurry, and continued down. He heard the front door open, then the few seconds it took for the spring to retract, followed by the click.

What was this place? He looked around him. The room he was in stank of tobacco, of sleep with unopened windows, of cheap perfume and stagnant air. The floor was scattered with grubby, crumpled sleeping bags—fourteen, maybe sixteen—with barely any room to walk between them. A single sink with a faucet was piled with dirty dishes. Unwashed mugs filled with cigarette butts lined the walls, a single electric kettle, a carton of teabags, and a jar of coffee perched on a shelf. A line was rigged from a cupboard to the curtain rod, on which were hung washed-out tights and underwear. Women lived here.

Benny opened the door a crack; he listened and looked, and opened it farther. Now there was just one more flight of stairs to go. He was about to step out when he heard a door open above him. He backed into the room, pulling the door to. Someone had stayed behind. A voice called, menacingly soft, "You should have known which side your bread was buttered on; you should have stuck by me, baby, bunking off like that, you stupid little idiot. Did you think we wouldn't catch up with you? Reckon you'll get impaled for this, *Miss Kovachev*; just like a butterfly—such a pity. You were doing so well, Nina. He trusted you. Vlad doesn't forgive treachery, especially when it involves his little girl." It was Don.

A bolt was drawn, and a key turned in a lock. Measured footsteps came down the stairs, passed his door, and continued to the bottom. Benny waited to hear the front door open. He crept out of the stinking room, paused, and risked peering over the banister to the hallway below. Don was standing as if in thought, his arms clasped around himself, enveloping his head, his fingers massaging his neck, shoulders and arms. Then, with a deep breath, he opened the front door and walked out, leaving the door slowly closing on the spring. *Click.*

17

BROKEN SPELLS

The day before the party, Raisa came over to stay the night. They practiced hard all day, and for once, the house was filled with girlish laughter. It was just after lunch that, her face full of smiles, Nettie responded to a beep on her cell phone. She checked her message. FOUND MISS K. BENNY. Her smiles vanished. She stared disbelievingly at the screen until the light went out. She flicked it on and read it again: FOUND MISS K.

"Everything okay?" asked Raisa.

There was a strange stillness about Nettie. She seemed transfixed, as though a magic spell had turned her to stone as she stared at her phone screen. Then she turned reassuringly. "I think so." Nettie didn't know why she said that. If everything was okay, why wasn't she filled with huge joy, and spinning around the room with excitement? Instead she sent back a text: COME TO ROUND TOWER.

Raisa noticed her fingers were trembling.

Benny was waiting when they arrived. He looked questioningly at Raisa. "It's fine," said Nettie. "She's my friend, Raisa. I told you about her. She can know whatever there is to know."

The three of them sat there in the Round Tower like the three monkeys, and Benny told his story.

"I was scared they'd come back, man. I asked her if she needed help. She told me to phone a bloke called Mike. I did. Said he'd be around in ten minutes, and then I scarpered. I heard police sirens in less than nine, but one thing, yeh? She was crying, an' all that, and saying, 'I didn't want her to know.' I think she meant you." His voice trailed away into a long silence.

No one moved. No one said anything, till at last, with a deep sigh, Nettie went to the drawer under the bed, pulled out the notebook, and gave it to Raisa. "Miss Kovachev wrote this. You told me you knew Bulgarian. Read it. Read it out loud. I need to know what it says."

See no evil, speak no evil, hear no evil.

Raisa opened the book and began to translate what had been written, there in the Round Tower.

. . . I was brought into your house by Don because he thought I was exactly the kind of person your father wanted to tutor his daughter; someone he could trust to teach you, Nettie—you, whom he adored with every fiber of his being, and me, who was in his power, and who he could be sure would not give away his secrets. But I found out that this was the man who had destroyed my sister Anna. This was Mr. Big. I tasted revenge. From then on, I didn't need Mike to encourage me. Now, nothing was more important than exposing Mr. Big. It became more important than you.

I, Nina Kovachev, had come into the house of my enemy. I would find out his secrets and destroy him.

All the lights and mirrors and chandeliers in the world could not penetrate the vampire darkness inside Vlad. His shadow spread across the land like the wings of death, luring his victims from as far away as my little village in Bulgaria; using his own brother, Charles Robart; using Kusa, Don, and others to traffic his human cargo; building all his wealth and power with the blood of poor, innocent, helpless, gullible girls like Anna and me.

Your father, Nettie, was one of the big ones—one of the godfathers of crime, but so powerful that no one had yet been able to get near him. Chiefs of police, immigration officers, solicitors, priests, judges, even teachers like Don—so many were on his payroll; so many had also been sucked into his deadly embrace. They were in the racket. Their rewards for being loyal to him were huge. The penalties for betrayal were terrible. It wasn't for nothing that they called him Vlad the Impaler.

"My father, my father, darling Daddy, so kind and generous; it can't be true!" Nettie's soul howled silently.

All afternoon, Raisa translated the notebook, while Benny stared silently out across the city, and Nettie curled up on the floor in a tight ball, her eyes sealed closed. She hadn't seen the evil, or spoken the evil, but now she heard the evil, and felt as if it was killing her, and she knew she was a child of it, a part of it, and must somehow face up to it. And as Raisa neared the end, Nettie felt as though all her life she had been wrapped in a silken cocoon which, throughout that afternoon, unwound until she stood like one naked; full of shame; exposed to the full truth.

I tried not to feel attached to you, but you were so like the little daughter I would like to have had. My child, too, came out of evil, and died before she could flower and find beauty. You could have been my daughter, full of innocence and curiosity; discovering the world and marveling at it. Soon, it became more important to me to educate you than to trap your father; to show you the beautiful world, and empower you to feel able to enter it in your own right; that one day you would be free and enter the world as Nettie; not Nettie, the crime lord's daughter.

But the time came when I knew I had to either tell Mike everything I had learned, or run away—disappear. I couldn't look into your trusting face each day knowing I was deceiving you; knowing that I now had enough knowledge to destroy your home, and the mother and father you loved.

I was a coward, Nettie. I ran away.

18

Through Knowledge to the Light of Truth

Regent Mansion shimmered as if made up of stardust. It reflected in the gleaming banisters of those scarlet staircases, across the marble floors, catching the light in shining vases and bronze statuettes. The crystal droplets in the chandelier sparkled like tears over the party that milled below. If evil could be seen in mirrors, whispered along corridors, heard behind closed doors, then every piece of brick, marble, and stone in the house knew about the evil that lived within it. But it also knew the love and the beauty; the innocence and hope. It saw Nettie running desperately to her great-aunt. Hadn't she talked about truth? She knew, didn't she?

"Why didn't you tell me?" Nettie accused her.

Great-aunt was dressed as a queen. She looked very, very far away, sitting regally upright on a thronelike chair, in the bay windows of her unlit room. She held the ends of a wafting cloak in her fingertips.

"It was not my business," she said in a voice that hardly seemed to come from her. "I was born to dance. That alone was my destiny."

"Peachy's child!" It was Mara.

Nettie whirled around. "Mara? Mara!" She rushed into the old dresser's arms and wept.

"*Ma pauvre*, my poor sweet little one," she crooned. "*Viens, viens avec moi*, come with me. All is not lost, *ma petite. Viens . . .*" And she led the girl as she would have led a lost lamb. Nettie wept a long time, until at last, as her sobbing decreased, Mara released her gently and went to the piano. Through a single note on the piano, Nettie could hear the solo violin which Raisa would play, and with quivering arms she began a slow sad dance.

"You see, Peachy's child, you will dance, and dance will be your redemption."

Nettie glided towards her great-aunt, until she knelt down on one knee, with bowed head. The queen raised her up, and embraced her. "My darling child, like Sleeping Beauty you have been woken from a sleep; the beautiful sleep of happy childhood, full of dreams, and hope. Your awakening has been a shock; the reality worse than any nightmare. But you will come through it; and one day, you will know that the fairies bestowed good wishes on you; the first most important thing was that you were happy, and you were truly loved. The second most important thing is that you will have taken charge of your own destiny; your own knowledge of right and wrong, good and bad. And third, by your own abilities and talents, you need never take anything tainted from anyone ever again. Now dance. You have a performance to prepare."

Peachy had organized a wonderful feast. Not only had all Vlad and Peachy's friends been invited, but the whole of Nettie's class, including their brothers and sisters. If only Nettie could have waved a magic wand and canceled everything, she would have. But there they were, all dressed in glittering clothes; excited, chattering, laughing, marveling, pointing, and noticing.

Fabulous trestle tables heaving with food were set out in the conservatory. Maids and valets in black and white hovered like sleek birds, carrying silver platters of canapés.

A boy band played for them, and they danced throughout the evening. Candles and fairy lights cast a magical glow, glimmering in their jewels, tossing reflections into the swimming pool as if the gold mosaic ceiling had become gleaming fish that darted and leaped in the water.

The guests spread out through the house and gardens; following candlelit paths, discovering spluttering braziers where white-hatted, white-aproned cooks tossed barbecued steaks, corn on the cob, stuffed peppers, and kebabs.

Among the marble pillars and clusters of palms, Nettie heard her name spoken softly. "Imagine Nettie living like this! My dad says no one can be so rich and be this side of the law. Did you see those diamonds her mother was wearing?" Another voice agreed. "Nettie's bracelet must be worth, like, a few quid. I'd say they were mixed sapphires and diamonds!"

"I hope she invites us to go skiing with her. I hear her father always takes over an entire hotel in Switzerland."

"It's to put up, like, all those servants and bodyguards." And they burst out laughing.

Nettie fell back into the shadows; hot, cold, tears, fury—all those passions overwhelmed. Never had she hated herself so much; how was it possible that she hadn't seen or understood what everyone else had?

"Where's Benny?" Nettie looked around for the one person who understood her. She hadn't seen him the whole evening, though all the staff had been invited to the party. But neither Benny nor his father was to be seen.

Suddenly her maid, Ella, was at her side. "Nettie, it's time for the performance! Your friend Raisa's waiting for you in your great-aunt's apartment. Miss Mara says you ought to get changed now. Everyone is going to the music room."

This was the climax of the party.

Mara dressed Nettie, just had she had dressed Great-aunt Laetitia throughout all those years of dancing. She brought out the white swan tutu all feathery and fluttery, and the little headdress with the princess's tiara, and more white feathers that drooped down on either side of Nettie's head. Finally, Nettie tied on her white silken pointe shoes.

Raisa wore a simple deep red velvet dress with a satin bodice. But it was not the Guarnerius violin she held in her hand; no matter how extraordinary it was, that instrument was Vlad's and, somehow, she couldn't bring herself to even touch it. She made an excuse that she preferred her own after all.

Down in the music room, the carpet at one end had been taken up to reveal the smooth polished oak floorboards on which Nettie would dance. Mara, in a black silk skirt and blouse, went to the piano, and Great-aunt sat to the side, upright and distant.

Nettie stepped to the front. The audience stretched before her, smiling encouragingly. Sitting on scattered cushions were all her school friends. A little behind to the center her mother and father, Peachy and Vlad, sat on gilt chairs, with their friends. Farther back still were as many of the staff who were free, but where were Benny and his father? Her eyes fruitlessly scanned the faces: Nanny, Ella, Paul, Cook, Swivel-Eyes, Ethan, Peckham, and Gimley; but no Baldwin, no Benny.

And Don! She had a moment of panic. Where was Don? How

could she dance if Don was there? She couldn't bear to see him ever again. But there was no Don.

Great-aunt tapped her long gold staff on the floor, indicating that the proceedings should begin. Nettie's panic gave way to a strange calm. Suddenly she knew what she must do. Nettie gazed upon her father and mother. People were amazed at her poise. She was no longer the child, Nettie, but a beautiful princess. Looking only at her parents, as if no one else was present, Nettie began to tell the story she would dance.

"Because I am dancing by myself, there is only me to tell you the story of *Swan Lake*, and you will have to imagine the handsome Prince Siegfried, who loved Odette the Swan Princess, and the dark magician who was as evil as any cruel tyrant there has ever been; as evil as Bluebeard; as evil as Vlad the Impaler and Count Dracula." Nettie's eyes seemed to stare straight into her father's soul.

She gave the signal, and Mara started to play the harplike chords from *Swan Lake*, whirling mysteriously up and down the keyboard.

"An evil magician has captured beautiful young girls, and turned them into swans. Among them is a Swan Princess called Nina."

"Nina? Surely, her name was Odette?" those who knew whispered in surprise.

Mara played the trembling, soulful music of *Swan Lake*; it seemed like rustling leaves in a night breeze, like water rippling on a lake. Nettie rose *en pointe*, her arms quivering as she began to dance and tell the story, stringing together all the steps she knew.

"A hunter is lost in the woods. By night, he comes to a mysterious moonlit lake, covered in a white mist. Suddenly, to his amazement, he sees a single white swan come in to land. Is he confused by the shifting mists, or does he see the shape of the swan changing . . . changing . . . into a beautiful young girl?"

Nettie glided forward to the center of the stage, and stood shimmering, making slight swanlike preening movements with her head. She mimed the moment that Prince Siegfried steps forward. " 'I love you,' he says. She falls back quivering and afraid, but his words reassure her and, using her arms with flowing gestures, she tells the prince that she is in the power of a wicked magician; that she can only be human between the hours of midnight and dawn. Other swans glide back to the lake. At that moment, the prince's friends rush in with their crossbows, ready to kill the beautiful creatures. 'No!' cries Nina, and springs in front of the flock, who are also girls the magician has captured. The men lower their weapons, as the Swan Princess mingles among the white swirling feathers of her distressed companions. The prince runs wildly among them, looking for her. With a soft, magical ripple of notes on a harp, Nina comes before him."

Mara ran her fingers up the piano, as if she played a harp. This was the cue for Raisa to lift the violin and tuck it under her jaw. She closed her eyes. A haunting, sad violin melody soared from under her bow as if enchanted, as if her own cheap violin was the beautiful Guarnerius; and Nettie began to dance the heartrending solo of despair and tragedy.

She danced to show her love; she danced to show how much she wished she could be freed from the spell, but it could never be. Every movement she made was limpid and swanlike; her arms flowed, and she moved with such delicate grace that tears came into people's eyes. "Now dawn is coming, and Nina/Odette is turning back into a swan. She flutters and trembles, gliding backwards in quickening bourrées, her arms outstretched pleadingly. 'Save me, save me!' " Before disappearing from the stage, Nettie turned and looked straight into her father's eyes. She pleaded for the lives of the Swan Princesses. "Please don't destroy these beautiful maidens."

The audience burst out with rapturous applause. Nettie came forward to give a deep curtsy the ballerina way. Only Nettie's father didn't applaud. He stared vacantly in front, his hands clasped, his eyes narrowed under a furious brow, while Peachy looked pale and transfixed. Nettie beckoned Mara and Raisa to acknowledge the ovation, then all of them curtsied deeply and respectfully before Nettie's teacher, Nettie's inspiration, Great-aunt Laetitia.

The applause, yells, and whistles continued. Nettie returned to take another curtsy. When she looked towards her father, his seat was empty. He had gone.

19

FINALE

Regent Mansion was empty once more. The mirrors, ornaments, furniture, paintings—all had been cleared away. All that was left were the empty rooms, the stripped staircases, the dusty marble floors, the emptied swimming pool, and the atrium around which the whole house had risen from bottom to top—the atrium, which was as hollow as a pitiless heart.

Nettie had wanted to say one last goodbye, and had come back to the house with Nanny. While Nanny waited in the hall, sitting on a single abandoned chair, Nettie climbed up floor by floor, walking in and out of rooms, remembering her innocence. There were some rooms she wouldn't enter. Neither her own, nor her parents' room. The pain was too intense. Even now, the tears flowed, as she knew that she might never feel so happy, so loved, ever again; they might never ever be together again as one family. Her father had gone— flown off in his jet, no one knew where. Yet again, Vlad the Impaler had gotten away. Peachy had retreated to Frithwood in a state of nervous collapse. The police wanted to interview her—the police wanted to interview everyone. The phone call Benny had made for Miss Kovachev had brought Mike and the police to rescue her. They had arrested Don, and cracked another racket. They would have taken in Mr. Baldwin, too, but he and Benny had gone—back to Barbados; that's what they told her. All that was left of Benny was a message from him, gleaming on her cell phone: BYE NETTIE. HPE ULL TLK 2 ME AGEN 1 DAY WEN U R FAMOUS. BENNY.

She stood at the side stairs leading to the Round Tower. She had left this room till last, but she couldn't leave without seeing it one more time. She began to climb. When she reached the door, she hesitated a second, then thrust it open. The room was empty, too. It had been stripped of all its specially made furniture—the round bed, the sofa, the shelves and tables, and the bath. She went into the bathroom and opened the cupboard. The back door was a little ajar. The back stairs disappeared into the darkness; down, down, down to where Benny had lived.

"Nettie!" A face emerged out of the darkness.

"Benny?" She ran forward joyfully.

"No, Nettie, it's me." Nina Kovachev came through the cupboard door.

Per Cognitionem ad Lucem Veritatis. From knowledge to the light of truth. Stardust.

As Nettie wept, Miss Kovachev asked her forgiveness for destroying her life. "But you will make a new one—and a good one. You must, so that I won't feel guilty forever."

"How shall I live?" Nettie cried despairingly. "I can't go back to school." She knew that everything she had ever had was because of evil. All her father's generosity was steeped in the blood of his victims.

"You will dance—and dancing will set you free of all of it. Your great-aunt tells me she has entered you for a scholarship into the Royal Ballet School. You will succeed; we know you will, and from now on, not a penny you take will be your father's. You will live with your great-aunt and Mara, until your mother is able to make her life again."

"And you?" asked Nettie. "Are you going home now?"

"Mike says I can go to university. Legit! Here in England. No more spying on people, no drugs and crime, and, one day, I will write my book. And, Nettie, I hope you and I will stay friends?"

A long time after, they left the Round Tower and descended the winding staircase with its oak banisters gathering dust. Nanny was waiting, and all three stepped out into the bright daylight leaving Regent Mansion forever. There was no butler to open the door, no chauffeur-driven limousine, no bodyguards. They walked through the park, allowing the green spaces and the sunlight in the trees to illuminate a new world. When they reached the gates at the far end, they made their way among the crowd to the underground.

POSTSCRIPT

Sometimes I dream I am walking along a dark road. Night falls as black as pitch; a night, brittle with frost. Diamond-hard constellations stud a leather-black sky. I'm so cold; I'm going to die.

Two lights, appear, heading towards me like a comet; a car. I don't try to thumb it down, as the beams sweep over me, catching me in their spotlight like a wild animal. It brakes violently to a stop. The car door opens.

"Nina? It's you, isn't it? Come on, get in. I'll give you a lift."